Return
to
Jade
Island

MANDY CASTO

For Id

"Many people will walk in and out of your life, but only true friends will leave footprints in your heart."
— Eleanor Roosevelt

CONTENT WARNING

Return to Jade Island contains themes related to the following: car-pedestrian accidents, classism, death, family estrangement, grief, maternal burnout, mental health issues, parental abandonment, parental rejection, and gun violence.

THE FIRST LETTER

September 1, 1974
Dear Mother,

I don't know where to start, but I guess stating the obvious and an apology is a good first step. I did not leave on very good terms, and I apologize for that. You may not be ready to hear me out over the telephone and I'm not sure I'm ready for that either, so I'm writing you this letter to explain myself. I very much hope that you read it.

I told you that I'm in love with Clark, but I haven't been able to fully express the magnitude of that love. It is so much more than the "puppy love" that you claim it to be. We've been best friends—practically each other's shadow—since the fifth grade, when we were partnered together for the school science fair. As we've grown up, our friendship has blossomed into something more. I can think of no better way to describe him than being my soulmate. He and I love the same music, the same books, and share the same dreams for our future. Clark even encourages my passion for writing. He gets me in a way nobody else does, and, he says the same thing about me.

What I didn't share with you is that we have been discussing marriage and having a family together as an inevitable step in our lives. Sure, we have also discussed graduating high school, going to college, and traveling around the world, too. But when we found out I was pregnant, it necessarily changed the timeline. Ideally, we would have finished out

7

school and then started our life together, building our family at home, but unfortunately, that wasn't an option. So we took the only option that we felt we had: leaving Jade Island to put a roof over our heads.

I don't want you to be under the impression that we don't understand our parents' concerns for us—we do. Honestly, I am concerned, too! I'm not so naive that I don't question whether we are making the best decision or the biggest mistake of our lives. You said that we are too young to become parents and that we haven't had time to explore the world like you did at my age. That may be true, but I won't ignore other motivations fueling your side of the argument, which is that you don't want me, your unwed, pregnant, seventeen-year-old daughter, to tarnish our family's reputation. I get it; ending this pregnancy is the much easier option for you. That isn't what Clark and I want, though. And what I don't understand is, knowing that, how you can proclaim to love me and yet still offer the ultimatum that has forced us to leave. I can think of nothing that my child could do for which I wouldn't be there for them.

I understand the arguments you made before we left. And while it hurts like hell, I want you to know that I forgive you for making me choose between all I've ever known and becoming a wife and a mother, which I've come to realize, since falling in love with Clark, is all I've ever wanted to be. I'd be lying if I didn't say that I'm devastated to start this next chapter of my life somewhere other than our home, but at the same time, I could not be more excited to meet this baby. He or she is going to bring our family so much joy, and I can't wait for that day.

Clark and I arrived yesterday at his cousin's house in San Fernando. It is a city just outside Los Angeles. I'm working on transforming his attic into a comfortable living space for us while Clark begins a new job that his cousin lined up for him in construction. It isn't his dream job, but it'll do for the meantime. This week I will start looking for work that I can do before the baby arrives.

I will miss you while we're gone. I just hope one day you can forgive me for making this choice and that we'll reunite as a family.

Love,
Ophelia

2015

CHAPTER ONE

Monday, June 29

Julianne was forty thousand feet in the air when it finally hit her: Eleanor Devereaux, "the Matriarch of Jade Island" as she was known at home, her grandmother and only living relative, was dead.

Julianne had been in the middle of the night shift at the field hospital when she got the text from an unknown number:

Call Richard. Urgent.

She recognized the Washington area code right away and put two and two together: something had happened to Grammy.

After finishing up with her patient, Julianne hurried down the narrow fluorescently lit corridor to the nearest exit, where she made all her phone calls. She rarely used the office that was assigned to her—a recently renovated interior storage closet fitted with a makeshift desk and a chair—which did not get cell service. The field hospital set up just outside Tehran had obviously not had enough time to prepare for the arrival of their latest recruits last month. She pulled up the text message and called the number back.

"Julianne?" a familiar voice said.

11

"Yes, this is her," Julianne answered.

"It's Richard Adams, your grandmother's friend," the voice said. Julianne remembered Richard well from her childhood, but he still introduced himself as if they'd just met.

"Hi, Richard. What's going on with Grammy?" Julianne spoke in her calm and reassuring doctor voice as she got straight to the point.

"Uh, well." Richard paused to clear his dry throat. "Yes, I'm at the hospital with your grandmother. The fact of the matter is we're in the ICU. She seems to have had a stroke. A pretty big one."

Julianne pinched the bridge of her nose between her thumb and forefinger and slowly crouched down toward the ground to steady herself. Despite her bubbling emotions, she found herself staying in doctor mode as she began to ask questions about her grandmother. At her request, Richard found a nurse who was able to give Julianne a more detailed update on her condition. Ms. Devereaux had been in a coma since she arrived at the hospital. Her advanced directive on file clearly stated she did not want drastic lifesaving measures in a dire situation such as this, so they were treating her palliatively, making her comfortable more than anything else. Unfortunately, her vitals had not shown significant improvement since she was admitted. At eighty-seven years old, her medical team was not optimistic she would pull through.

The nurse handed Richard the phone after answering all of Julianne's questions. "Julianne, I'm here. What can I do?"

"I will get on the next flight," said Julianne.

"I respect your wishes to come here, but even if you left right now, I'm not sure she—"

"I have to come, Richard. I'll send you my flight information as soon as I have it." With that, she hung up, sensing a tidal wave of emotion rising from her gut, up her spine, and into her cheeks. Talking on the phone a minute longer would have undoubtedly resulted in tears and a runny nose for the rest of the day. There would be plenty of time for that later; right now, she needed to remain calm before she left work.

As a sliver of the bright orange sun emerged above the easterly horizon, Julianne took a moment to collect herself. The stillness of dawn brought her back to the conversation she had had with her grandmother a few months before, which had led her to the Middle East. They were having their regular Sunday night check-in over the phone when Julianne opened the email containing a job offer to work with Doctors without Borders.

"Well, there's no question. You have to take it," her grandmother said.

This opportunity would be life changing, there was no question. At the same time, it would take her far away from her grandmother. While Julianne had not been back to her childhood home on Jade Island in nearly ten years, Grammy still visited her anytime she was on the mainland. Plus, there was comfort in knowing she was never more than a car ride away.

"I don't know, Grammy . . ." Julianne replied. She had applied to work with Doctors without Borders but hadn't seriously contemplated it. After she graduated, she settled into a position at a Seattle-based community clinic. She was even able to keep the same apartment she'd had in medical school.

"Julianne, you did not work *that* hard and graduate at the *top* of your class to live your life as an overworked and underutilized health center . . . *peon*." Eleanor was annoyed at the thought of her granddaughter working beneath her talent.

"It's not *that* bad," Julianne quietly retorted. "And what about . . . you?" she asked, trying not to imply the obvious.

"Dear, you have not been here to take care of me in ten years. I am perfectly capable of taking care of myself, and I'm offended that you would think otherwise."

Well, that was that. If Julianne was being honest with herself, she was excited about the prospect of working abroad—of meeting new challenges and having a change of scenery. She didn't have a partner or even a pet tying her down. Plus, if Julianne turned down the offer, she knew from experience that she would never hear the end of it. Her grandmother's palpable disappointment would have made their Sunday night check-ins rather uncomfortable. For Julianne, at least.

So she quit her job at the clinic downtown, boxed up her apartment to put into storage, and joined a Doctors without Borders medical team, which was quickly deployed to Tehran. She felt barely settled into her new surroundings when she received the fateful phone call from Richard.

Julianne booked the next flight bound for Seattle. Less than three hours later, she boarded a flight to London, the first stop on her journey back to Jade Island. She sat down in her assigned window seat in the back of the plane and shoved the baby blue JanSport backpack she'd had since high school under the row in front of her. Just as she was about to switch her phone into airplane mode, the hospital called.

Ms. Devereaux had died.

Just as Julianne ended the call and prepared her phone for the flight, she became distracted by a woman and her young daughter taking their seats next to her. Julianne guessed that the woman, wearing a blue-and-white-patterned chiffon hijab, was approximately her age, mid to late twenties.

The girl, who had a shiny black braid down the middle of her back and wore a Mickey Mouse pajama set, held on to her oversized headphones with one hand and carried a stuffed monkey in the other.

"Look at the television, Mama!" the girl exclaimed excitedly at her mother in the most adorable British accent Julianne had ever heard. She dropped the stuffed toy and pointed toward the screen in the back of the headrest as her mother adjusted the girl's seat belt. The girl was five years old, six at most. The woman gave a quick apologetic glance at Julianne before looking upward with mild exasperation. She then leaned close to her daughter and whispered something in her ear while gently stroking her braided hair. The young girl turned toward Julianne and mouthed, "Sorry." Julianne answered with a polite grin.

She closed her eyes and took several long, deep breaths to keep her emotions in check. The last thing she wanted to do was to become a blubbering mess—or, worse yet, start bawling like a baby in front of her cheerful young seatmate. Instead, she plugged in the headphones the attendant handed her and searched the in-flight movies for a distraction. She immediately landed on *When Harry Met Sally*, one of her mom's favorite movies and one that she had watched with her mom and Grammy nearly a dozen times growing up. It was the closest thing to soul food she knew.

It wasn't until several hours later—after the movie had ended, the flight attendants had come through with their snack carts, and the little girl had fallen sound asleep in her mother's lap—that the stark realization of her grandmother's death hit Julianne for the first time.

This time, in the darkness of the cabin, she let the tears flow.

CHAPTER TWO

After enduring two long flights and nearly an entire twenty-four hours of travel, Julianne embarked on the next leg of her journey and possibly the hardest bit thus far. Having packed everything in her carry-on luggage, she hurried past fellow passengers as they nervously hovered around the baggage carousels and out to the arrivals concourse at Seattle-Tacoma International Airport. A thin layer of clouds broke up the direct beam of sunlight that hit her when she passed through the sliding glass doors. She squinted down at her watch to check the time just as a white BMW convertible crept up and parked along the curb right in front of her. Richard slowly pushed the driver's-side door open and, with some noticeable effort, rose to his feet. He stretched out his back before walking around to meet Julianne at the open trunk.

Julianne loaded her bags into the small trunk before giving her grandmother's oldest friend an obligatory hug. His embrace felt familiar yet different; he had lost some height and body mass in his old age. He held on to her for a beat longer than she felt was necessary, but she didn't pull away. This loss must have been as hard on him as it was on her, probably even more so—he and Grammy had been thick as thieves for as long as she could remember. As she climbed into the passenger seat, she was knocked back into her seat by a waft of Calvin Klein's Obsession, Grammy's perfume of choice for the past fifty years. Julianne realized that there was no use in trying to avoid it: this trip back was going to force her down memory lane whether she liked it or not.

"Thanks for picking me up, Richard. It was completely unnecessary, though. I could have rented a car," Julianne said as she stretched the seat belt across her body.

"Ah, well, your grandmother would have socked me right here in the arm if I didn't see to it that you got home safe." Richard pointed to his flexed arm.

Julianne pondered the word *home*. What a foreign concept to her now. She hadn't considered Jade Island—the place where she was born and raised—to be her home in over a decade. She didn't have a home on the island anymore. Since she'd left, she didn't feel as though she had a home anywhere, including her last apartment in Seattle. But Richard didn't need to know that.

"I'm sorry you didn't get to say goodbye, kiddo," Richard said as he merged Eleanor's convertible back into traffic. Richard didn't own a car of his own, claiming that he didn't need one on the island and rarely had a reason to leave. Once Eleanor had given her friend the spare set of keys to her car and an open invitation to drive it whenever necessary, Richard didn't plan on ever buying a car again.

"Me, too." After an awkward pause, she added, "She's at peace, though. That's all that matters, right?" That's what people said in situations like this. As a physician, she had heard that line more times than she could count. Julianne looked out the passenger window as Richard veered the car onto the northbound expressway. The radio was off, and they rode to the soothing soundtrack of her intermittent yawns and the tires surfing the pavement beneath them. Despite the cars, buildings, and billboards whizzing by, the world actually felt still for a moment.

A few minutes into the drive, Richard broke the silence. "Your grandmother was still raising hell up until, you know, her final days."

"Oh, there's no surprise there," Julianne replied. As Richard went on about Eleanor's long-standing argument with the deputy mayor over the "repugnant pink pansies" that were planted in hanging baskets around town, Julianne's attention drifted back to her last few phone conversations with her grandmother, which had been more sporadic since she left for Tehran. Grammy was in terrific shape for a woman almost in her nineties, but Julianne had begun to detect subtle signs of dementia during their phone conversations over the past few months. She pleaded with her grandmother to see a doctor for a checkup the last time they talked, but going to the doctor when one felt perfectly fine seemed completely unnecessary according to Eleanor. Everyone knew that what Eleanor said was final, and only a few bold individuals (including the deputy mayor) had the courage to argue with her. Some called her set in her ways; others called her flat-out stubborn. Being more forceful on the topic would have only driven them further apart, which Julianne didn't want. After all, they were already six thousand miles apart geographically.

After an uneventful ferry ride from Port Forrester, they finally reached Jade Island, Julianne's childhood home. The island was one of several that rose above the icy-cold waters of Puget Sound, just off the coast of Washington State. The tiny island sloped upward from the flat northeast end—home to the island's marina and ferry terminal—to the southwest edge, where rocky bluffs and evergreens stood hundreds of feet above sea level. The bluffs, which overlooked the rest of the island below, were dotted with homes that many tourists referred to as "charming chateaus" and "marvelous mansions." One of these Julianne used to call "home."

Julianne had successfully stayed away from the house where she grew up ever since she went off to college. Eleanor would visit her on campus from time to time, and they would meet in Port Forrester for birthdays and a few holidays. Eleanor never shamed her granddaughter for leaving or even asked her to come back, already knowing the answer to that question. As Richard turned left on the road that looped around the island and would eventually bring them to her grandmother's house, feelings of guilt began to seep into Julianne's consciousness. *I should not have left Grammy to live on her own. Had I just stayed, I could have taken Grammy to the doctor and maybe prevented this.* As a physician, she knew better than to follow this line of thinking. She quickly rationalized that a trip to the doctor weeks ago probably wouldn't have prevented the stroke. To live to be her grandmother's age and to go so quickly was a gift. Still, it was unfathomable to Julianne, as it soon would be to the entire island community, that the unflappable Eleanor Harris Devereaux went so quickly and with no warning.

CHAPTER THREE

Eleanor's home was one of only a few perched high on the southern cliffs. The house closest to Eleanor's belonged to Alex and Bethany, a fortysomething couple who moved to the island five years ago. As rain clouds moved overhead, blocking out the sunlight Bethany had been soaking up earlier that day, she watched Eleanor's BMW climb the steep and curvy driveway up to the house. From her screened-in porch, she recognized Richard, Eleanor's friend and amiable owner of the bookshop in Jade Island Square, as the driver and then noticed a young brunette in the passenger seat. The woman looked strangely familiar. She had seen her somewhere before, but she couldn't put her finger on it.

Over the years, Bethany had become very well-acquainted with her elderly neighbor, known to the locals as the Matriarch of Jade Island. Bethany loved being outside and spent most of the year on her enclosed porch, which had a perfect view of the bay on one side and Eleanor's home on the other. From time to time, she'd catch Eleanor's attention through the large windows of her study and enthusiastically wave her over for afternoon tea, which her stately neighbor often accepted. They would pass those afternoons laughing and gossiping about the locals over tea and macarons until the sun went down or Alex arrived home from meeting with clients, whichever came first.

On this day, however, Bethany sensed that something was wrong. She wanted to chalk it up to the ominous clouds that had quickly moved in, but she couldn't help but notice that Eleanor's home was unusually dark and that Richard had been coming and going from her neighbor's garage more often than usual.

She paced around for over an hour before deciding to walk over to her neighbor's house to find out for herself. It was raining steadily now, so she threw on her Wellies and grabbed an umbrella to keep her perfectly styled hair in place as she ran across both yards. She jogged up the stairs of Eleanor's grand porch, then took a moment to collect herself, running a hand over her straightened bleached-blond hair and across her clothes down to her thighs. She knocked and waited a few moments before the young woman answered.

"May I help you?" Julianne asked. *Whew,* Bethany thought to herself, *this girl has seen better days.*

"Hi, there. I'm Bethany, Eleanor's—"

"Ah, you're Grammy's next-door neighbor," Julianne interjected. "I'm Julianne, her granddaughter." She opened the door wider and gestured for Bethany to come inside. Bethany set down her umbrella and sidestepped into the foyer.

Bethany recognized the young woman immediately when they both stepped into the light. Although they had never met, Bethany had studied the giant portrait of a seventeen-year-old Julianne that hung in Eleanor's study enough times to paint the portrait herself. "Right! Oh, your grandmother has told me a great deal about you." Bethany paused. She didn't want to pry into why Julianne was in town for the first time in what must have been a decade. Julianne saved her from doing so.

"Well, um, I have some unfortunate news." Julianne

tilted her head sideways.

"Oh, no . . ." Bethany gave a knowing and sympathetic look. *I knew it,* she thought to herself.

"Yes, I'm afraid. She suffered a stroke, and she didn't recover."

Bethany raised her hand to cover her mouth, then, after a moment's hesitation, she spread both arms wide to wrap them around a seemingly impervious Julianne. "I'm so sorry to hear that," she said, giving her a tight squeeze before pulling away.

Julianne looked at the floor to keep her emotions at bay—something she had mastered over the years. "Thank you. You'll be seeing me around for another week or two as I . . . figure things out."

"Of course," Bethany replied. During one of their afternoon gossip sessions, Eleanor had revealed that Julianne was her only living heir. Her husband had been gone for decades, and her daughter and son-in-law—Julianne's parents—had passed away years ago in a tragic car accident. "Well, I am just a few steps away." She pointed to the modern brick farmhouse next door. "If you need anything, please, just come on over. Okay?"

"That's very kind, thank you," Julianne said. She started toward the door.

"I can bring you some dinner later if—"

Julianne cut her off gently midsentence. "I'm good for this evening, but thank you." Bethany got the sense that Julianne was uncomfortable, so she gave her a courteous nod and a quick smile, then shuffled out the front door.

The rain had softened into a light drizzle. As Bethany walked back to her house, she thought about Eleanor's pantry, which usually consisted of potato chips, Boost shakes, and ginger cookies. Eleanor was well known on the island, but certainly not for her culinary skills. In fact, she was often seen dining out around the island with friends and neighbors and avoiding her own kitchen.

Wanting to appear helpful, Bethany decided to take it upon herself to go to the market and buy some groceries for Julianne. Maybe she would bake her some brownies, too. Then Julianne would invite her in and they would quickly bond over some tantalizing stories about the Matriarch of Jade Island. If nothing else, it would quench Bethany's thirst for some human interaction.

As soon as Julianne closed the door behind Bethany, she slowly marched up the marble staircase to her childhood bedroom. Richard had brought her suitcase upstairs and placed it at the foot of her four-poster bed. She looked around and noticed that Grammy had not touched a thing since she'd gone off to college. Julianne caught her disheveled reflection in the mirror. No wonder the neighbor looked at her with such sympathy. She'd had every intention of taking a shower to wash off the past twenty-four hours of travel. Instead, she plopped down on the bed and let her emotions wash over her. She cried until there were no tears left and there was nothing but sleep.

THE SECOND LETTER

December 30, 1974
Dear Mother,

I hope that this letter finds you well. I had hoped we would be able to see each other during the holidays, but I know that this is always a busy time of year for you with all the charitable work that you do. And we weren't able to travel. As the newest man on the crew, Clark didn't receive much time off between the holidays this year. He tells me it won't be so bad once he has put in his time and rises through the ranks. I told him that all that matters is that he's home for the holidays and special occasions once the baby arrives. We'll make everything else work.

I do have some great news to share. My doctor ordered an ultrasound and we learned we're having a baby boy! I really can't wait for him to arrive. Of course I want to meet our son, but if I'm being honest, pregnancy is a weary and lonely road. I was pretty miserable during the first trimester (my doctor said that was normal), but I'm afraid this second one hasn't been much better. I continue to have morning sickness, which should just be called "sickness" at this point because it seems to last well into the afternoon more days than not. I live on a minimal diet of ginger ale, chicken noodle soup, and saltines. Mint chocolate chip ice cream is my current remedy of choice. My doctor has encouraged me to stay home and rest for now. I guess I don't have much of an option. It is difficult to find work in this condition. I would like to contribute to our household income, but Clark is making sure that I am following the doctor's orders.

You would be so proud of Clark—and his parents would be, too. He is working so hard. Even so, he still makes time to take me on dates every so often. We haven't ventured out too far from our street yet. Los Angeles has so much to see. At the same time, what we have seen isn't quite what I imagined it would be. It is hot and dry, for one. And there are so many people here! The air is thick and almost smoky some days with something the news meteorologist calls smog. We haven't been to Hollywood yet, but I can't wait to walk along the Walk of Fame! (If I find Lauren Bacall's star, I will take a picture and send it to you!) I also want to go to the Santa Monica Pier, the Griffith Observatory, and the famous Hollywood sign!

I get excited whenever I think about sightseeing around our new home, but what I am looking forward to most is our wedding. Clark and I are planning for sometime in early February, before the baby arrives. It will be a small ceremony here in L.A., and we would love for our family to attend. We haven't spoken to Clark's parents since we moved. He says it doesn't bother him, but I don't entirely buy it. I know that things were tense this summer, but I'd hoped that they would have come around by now. I'm still hopeful they will have a change of heart once the baby arrives. If you see them, please give them our best.

Love,
Ophelia

CHAPTER FOUR

Tuesday, June 30

Julianne entered Grammy's house through the front door. The house was pitch dark except for a sliver of light coming from Grammy's study at the back of the house. She cautiously moved through the grand foyer, past the sitting room and the kitchen, until she reached the door of the study, which was slightly ajar. From the other side of the closed door she heard voices, voices she would recognize from a mile away. It was her parents and Grammy. She cracked the door open and saw her grandmother sitting in her leather armchair with a glass of white zinfandel in one hand and a puzzle piece in the other. As she worked on one of her jigsaws, Julianne's parents just relaxed on the couch across the room, smiling lovingly at each other. Her father's arm was draped around her mother's shoulder as she leaned into him. The melodic notes of Grammy's favorite musician, John Coltrane, played softly in the background. Everyone seemed so happy.

Julianne's weak voice called into the room. "Hello?" but no one acknowledged her. She took a step farther into the room to get a better look at their faces. Upon closer inspection, she noticed her parents and grandmother had way fewer wrinkles, and her father had a full head of hair, not like she remembered him. This wasn't today, and it wasn't even ten years ago . . . she had stepped back in time. She walked closer to her parents and waved her hands to get their attention. Their gazes remained fixed on each other.

"Mom? Dad?" she choked out, but they didn't hear her. They couldn't hear her.

Suddenly, Julianne heard sounds coming from the kitchen. Cupboard doors shutting, dishes rattling, and a tea kettle whistling. There was never anyone else inside the house other than the four of them.

Who could be in the kitchen?

As soon as Julianne stepped outside the study to investigate the noises, the door slammed behind her.

BANG!

Julianne jolted awake at the noise of a kitchen cupboard door slamming shut downstairs. Bright light poured into the room through the white lace curtains that she had picked out when she was thirteen. It took her a moment to remember where she was. As soon as she did, she propped her head up and looked down toward the foot of the bed. She was still wearing the jeans and T-shirt that she wore when she arrived on the island. One by one, the events from the days before trickled back into her memory.

She flung her head backward onto the pillow and held her watch up to her face. It was eight thirty-one. *Must be morning.* As she reached for her phone, which was lying on the bed next to her, she heard more sounds from the kitchen downstairs. Julianne thought she could hear two people talking. Unlike her dream, the muffled cadence of these voices was less familiar.

In addition to multiple missed calls and texts from her college roommate and best friend, Jenny, her phone revealed that she had been asleep for nearly fifteen hours. Not enough to catch the jet lag she would have in the days to come, but a good start. She felt the warmth of the sun grazing her back as she propped herself up on her side. She took a deep breath. *What did Grammy always used to say?* "A new day for renewed strength," Julianne whispered to herself.

Even though she had no clue who was in the house with her, Julianne refused to go downstairs before taking a shower. It was likely Richard, but no matter who it was, she would not be subjecting them to her thick matted hair, dirty clothing, and overwhelming musty odor. So instead of investigating the sounds below, she unpacked her suitcase and opted for a nice long shower in her en suite bathroom.

Forty-five minutes later, a refreshed Julianne entered the kitchen to find Richard and the next-door neighbor cooking up a large breakfast. "Good morning," Julianne said. As soon as the words were out of her mouth, she realized how weary she sounded. While she felt refreshed from a night of undisrupted sleep and the hot shower, she still felt the remnants of the tears that had sent her into that deep slumber.

Bethany gave her a smile, but keenly sensing that Julianne was not a fan of physical displays of affection, she kept her distance for the time being. A much more oblivious Richard, however, approached Julianne and wrapped her in a big embrace. Julianne took a deep breath in and was, once again, transported back to her childhood. Richard's flannel shirt smelled of Cheer, the same laundry detergent that Grammy used. "How are you doing this morning, Julianne?"

"I'm okay," she said once he'd released her. "I think the sleep helped."

"Good, I'm glad to hear it," Richard said, a hint of relief in his voice. Bethany crossed the kitchen and, unable to help herself, reassuringly took Julianne's hand.

"I hope you don't mind, but I bought you some groceries. I brought them over yesterday afternoon, and Richard let me in," she said.

"Oh, that was so thoughtful." Julianne turned toward Richard. "Wait, how long have you been here?"

"Well, I came over yesterday afternoon to check on you. You were out like a light, so I decided to stay in case you woke up and, uh, needed anything."

"Oh, wow. Well, thank—" Julianne started to say before Richard waved her off.

"Not a big deal. I just rested my head on the couch in your grandmother's study. It's actually pretty comfy for a big guy like me." Julianne was about to reply and reassure him that she could take care of herself, but she stopped. He was only trying to be supportive and likely doing what he thought Grammy would want him to do in this situation.

Bethany walked over to the stove to continue frying what smelled like home fries with onions and peppers. "We knew you'd be awake sooner or later, so we thought we'd put a little meal together this morning. It's almost finished!" She gestured for Julianne to take a seat at the kitchen table. Julianne walked over to the ornate mahogany kitchen table that sat off to the side and poured herself some coffee from the carafe. As she sat down, where she had sat for breakfast with Grammy and her parents on so many mornings, she took in her surroundings while she watched Richard and Bethany finish making breakfast. It reminded her of when her parents would cook breakfast on the weekends.

Both of Julianne's parents were early risers, and every so often they would walk down to the corner market as soon as it opened to gather ingredients to make a large breakfast for the four of them. Julianne would wake up to the sound of eighties pop music playing on the radio as her parents made Julianne's favorites from scratch: banana pancakes, scrambled eggs, and home fries mixed with onions and peppers. The four of them would sit down and enjoy their feast as they were softly serenaded by the likes of Hall and Oates, Prince, and Madonna. Then Julianne would clean up before she and her dad would go outside to play around the island while her mom and Grammy would go shopping in the square or work on a puzzle in the study. Those particular mornings, as simple as they once seemed, were now the memories that Julianne's heart ached for the most.

"You are going through a lot, so we wanted to do what little we could to help out," said Bethany as she walked over to the table with multiple platters of food. Waffles, bacon, biscuits, home fries, and fresh fruit . . . She had to admit it was a welcome sight. Since May, many of her breakfasts had consisted primarily of flatbread, jam, and halim. They were tasty, but just not as satisfying as a home-cooked meal.

"This is great, but you . . . you didn't need to do all of this," Julianne said. She wanted to set boundaries right off the bat and make sure Richard and Bethany knew that she was fine without their help. She had practically been on her own for a decade. Self-sufficiency was her MO.

Bethany and Richard glanced briefly at each other and, if Julianne didn't know better, shared a smirk in response. "Don't mention it," Richard said, looking serious. "We are honored to be here for you. It's what your grandmother would have wanted." He squeezed Julianne's arm as he sat down next to her. Bethany settled into the seat across from her, where her mom used to sit.

Julianne stared at the food she had piled on her plate.

"Is something the matter?" Bethany asked.

"Appetite just isn't what it normally is." Julianne reached for her mug and took a sip. Even without a strong appetite, her body craved coffee—an addiction she'd developed during her days at the University of Washington. For all the unknowns her life had thrown her, her caffeine addiction had yet to fail her.

Richard dabbed his mouth with his napkin and spoke quietly. "Now, let's take everything one step at a time. Okay, kiddo?"

Bethany gently sniffled, trying to hold back the tears that were emerging in the corners of her eyes. She chimed in. "Yes, Richard's right. You said you'd be around for another week or two, right?" she asked.

Julianne nodded. "Yes, but—"

"Good. So you have time. And we are going to help you. Richard was telling me earlier that he has some help at the bookstore this summer, and I have a pretty open schedule."

"I can't ask you guys to—" Julianne started.

"Nonsense," Richard said. "Eleanor has been my steadfast friend for the past thirty years, ever since I showed up on this island with a tiny dream of opening that bookstore. You think that I was able to start it up and keep it running all these years by myself? I owe a lot of it to her. She helped me countless times over the years, and this is my chance to pay her back." Julianne could tell he was not going to back down.

Richard had made a similar speech when she first turned down the recruitment offer to become a travel doctor. Eleanor wanted her granddaughter to expand her horizons and take advantage of the opportunity to travel the world, so she enlisted the help of her oldest pal to persuade Julianne to take the job. Julianne felt horrible about leaving her grandmother on her own, but at the same time, she wasn't ready to return to the island. And Richard promised he would be there to take care of her until Julianne came back. Sure enough, he'd kept his word.

"Everything we do is in steps. And how do we take steps?" Richard asked, leading up to another one of Eleanor's famous sayings.

"One step at a time," Julianne said, a small smile forming on her lips.

"Right. Now, then, the first thing we want to do is locate your grandmother's will," said Richard. Bethany nodded along enthusiastically.

"All right. I will work on that today. It's probably in her study."

"I'll help you look for it," said Bethany. "Is there

anything else you would *like* to do today?"

Julianne took a moment to think, then said, "Yes. Actually, I think I'd just like to get out of the house."

Bethany was hoping she'd say that. It gave her a great idea.

CHAPTER FIVE

Jade Island had always held a special place in Melissa Santana's heart. After her brisk morning walk, she sat down to catch her breath on a park bench facing Jade Square Park. The park was a green space about the size of a football field in the center of town, encased by four one-lane roads with restaurants and small businesses that all faced one another. She took a deep breath and took in the familiar surroundings. *This place has not changed,* she thought. The streetlamps were still adorned with hanging baskets bursting with vibrant shades of coral, saffron, and vermilion. Children chased each other around the concrete fountain that stood tall in the center of the park, as parents looked on with watchful eyes from nearby benches. Even the shops and restaurants looked nearly identical despite a touch-up paint job here and there. She looked over her shoulder at the stores she'd frequented the most as a young teenager: Trixie's Trinkets, the Book Cellar, and Jade Island's Ice Cream & Soda Shoppe. Seeing these stores transported the thirty-three-year-old back in time to the first time she'd vacationed on the island.

She had just turned fourteen, and her dad's partner at his Seattle law firm had recently purchased a house on the island. Felipe (or Fel, as he liked to be called) and his sophisticated wife, Margaret (one of the few people who called her husband by his given name), had invited Melissa's family to spend the Fourth of July week with them and their sons, Chris and Charlie. Melissa's parents, both lawyers and self-proclaimed workaholics, rarely broke away from their clients to take Melissa and her two older brothers on vacation. It was a rare treat to go away for a short amount of time let alone an entire week. Even as a teenager, Melissa knew not to take this special getaway for granted.

Most of what Melissa remembered about that week was her, happily following the boys around without a care in the world. She no longer recalled anything that could possibly tarnish that perfect week in her mind, like her oldest brother, Mark, pushing her off the dock into the freezing cold water or the dozens of bug bites that she covered with calamine lotion on the drive home. Instead, she closed her eyes and heard the squeaks and squeals of dolphins chatting across the bay as the five teenagers tandem-kayaked around the island. Her face beamed thinking about their many foot and bicycle races to the square to get milkshakes after dinner. She felt the hot sand under her bare feet as they played volleyball at the beach. Melissa saw the vivid pattern of stars that she watched every night, shining brilliantly above her, as she listened to the waves brush up against the rocky shoreline. And she even felt her heart race the way it did whenever Chris's hand brushed against hers as they sat next to each other at the breakfast table each morning.

Melissa's family would come back a handful more times when she was in high school, and once when she was in college, but never for long enough. They'd visit the island when Fel and Margaret were there and, on a couple of occasions, when they were back in the city. As a way to try to manifest a future on the island, Melissa made an effort to get to know the neighbors, which was much more than Fel and Margaret did. She was even asked to babysit for the girl across the street, Julianne, one week when her family left town unexpectedly. Margaret insisted that their friends and family members get as much enjoyment out of the home as they did, especially in the summer months, when the island was ever-so-briefly cloaked in sunshine. Melissa was grateful that her parents took them up on that offer because, over time, Jade Island became her favorite escape from the real world.

Melissa came back to the island multiple times with Chris, but that was years later as his girlfriend, fiancée, and eventually wife. The last time the couple vacationed here, they had just learned she was pregnant with their first child. She remembered spending that week thinking up baby names on the beach (if it was a girl, they would name her Lily, after Melissa's favorite flower, the Asiatic lily), planning where they were going to put the bassinet in their room, and shopping for baby clothes. They had so much to look forward to.

Melissa's life had changed so much since then. But wherever life took her, she could always count on Jade Island to remain the same and give her a hearty dose of nostalgia whenever she returned. She had only been on the island since the night before, and she felt her heart exploding with happy memories. *Slow down and savor the present,* she told herself. There would be plenty of time to reminisce over the next two weeks.

Melissa opened her eyes and came back to the present. The clock at the top of the street post read it was ten minutes to the hour. Soon, the shops around the square would open and the area would become flooded with tourists. Although Melissa was technically vacationing on the island, too, she much rather considered herself to be a local. She rose to her feet, remembering why she'd walked down from the house in the first place: to grab the essentials for any relaxing summer day: an iced coffee and some books to take her mind off reality as much as possible. She couldn't wait to officially begin her vacation. First stop: Neptune's Cafe.

At the corner of Main Street and Pine Street—two roads that served as a partial perimeter of Jade Square Park—locals and tourists alike flocked to Neptune's Cafe. Bells jingled and a blast of chilly air-conditioning gave Melissa immediate goose bumps as she opened the door to the coffee shop.

Melissa loved going to Neptune's, a cafe in a converted 1950s Craftsman-style house that sat just outside the northwest corner of the square. Over the years, she'd developed the habit of walking down to the coffee shop at sunrise each morning with a book or fashion magazine, ordering a caramel latte, and then settling herself on the shaded side patio, where she could watch the center of town come alive with bustling tourists and locals. As Melissa approached the cafe, she noticed that the owners had expanded the patio and built an addition on the back of the house, signaling that business must still be good.

When she walked in the front door, it was surprisingly quiet. She didn't see a soul, and the only noise she heard was the faint sound of bossa nova streaming from one of the back sitting rooms. Each of the refurbished rooms was decorated thematically by decade. Her brothers' favorite room was in the back—a bedroom that was converted into a wood-paneled eighties-style lounge, complete with *Ms. Pac-Man* and *Asteroids* game consoles. Chris had always loved sitting in the vinyl bean bag chairs in the nineties room, which was plastered floor to ceiling with some of his favorite movie posters, like *Terminator 2: Judgment Day*, *Reservoir Dogs*, and *Fight Club*. Her parents' favorite was the retro seventies room, with its record player and pea green couches that smelled of patchouli. She loved them all.

Her daydreaming was suddenly interrupted by a ruggedly handsome fortysomething peering around the open door of a storage room. "Hey there," he said, as he stepped behind the counter.

"Good morning," Melissa replied.

"What can I get for ya?" he asked, looking into her eyes. She found herself unable to form words as his baby blues pierced hers.

Melissa broke eye contact as soon as she could and focused her gaze on the menu board above his eyeline. Even though she wasn't looking at him, she could still feel his stare. "Just an iced coffee, please. Medium."

What a boring order, she thought to herself, so she added, "And why don't you throw in a shot of espresso and some caramel while we're at it." *There, that's more exciting.*

"Yeah, absolutely," he said, his words flowing melodically. He held her gaze for an extra moment as the corner of his lip curled into a grin. As he turned toward the espresso maker, Melissa noticed his toned arms, which were covered in tattoos. She had never been into tattoos, but she found herself unable to take her eyes off his.

"How's your morning going?" he asked. He must have noticed her staring.

"Oh, pretty good so far. Yours?"

"Not bad, not bad. Hoping to get out on the water this afternoon after my shift."

"Oh, cool. Do you live here on the island?" Melissa asked. The barista tossed his head. When he didn't respond immediately, Melissa thought, *Why did you ask that? Too personal, Mel.* She couldn't imagine a coffee shop barista of his age living in one of the million-dollar homes on the island, yet her curiosity had gotten the better of her.

Eventually, he said, "Nah, I'm just hanging out for the summer." He placed a lid on the paper cup and pushed it across the counter. His smile cut through any embarrassment she'd felt.

Melissa looked down at the cup and smiled

sheepishly back. As she paid, she looked at his nametag.

"Well, *J.D.*, I hope you have a fun afternoon. Thanks for the coffee."

"Will do . . ." he said slowly, signaling he wanted her name in return.

"Melissa."

"Will do, *Melissa*. Have a great day." He winked at her before walking back to the storage room behind the counter. As Melissa turned toward the door, she rubbed her arms to try to smooth down the goose bumps that had returned.

She pushed the front door open and put the straw to her lips to take a sip. As she sipped, chills rushed through her body. She couldn't tell what had caused it—the ice-cold beverage in her hand or the fact that it had been years since she'd had any sort of flirtatious interaction with a man. Whatever it was, her footsteps felt a little lighter as she walked down the steps and down the street toward the bookstore.

CHAPTER SIX

After breakfast, Richard left Eleanor's house to open the bookshop while Julianne and Bethany began cleaning up the kitchen. Once the pots, pans, and dishes were rinsed and in the sink, Julianne threw the kitchen towel over the faucet and mentally declared that the kitchen was tidy enough for the time being. As the world's highest-functioning procrastinator, Julianne was content with leaving the rest of it for later . . . probably late at night when she couldn't fall asleep.

"Well then, are we ready to go?" Bethany asked. At breakfast, Bethany had proposed taking an adventure around the island, starting with a hike to the beach on the north end. Julianne wasn't sold on the idea at first, but it only took Bethany a few minutes and her West Coast charm to persuade her.

"Oh, c'mon! The forecast shows we are not going to see better weather than today. Not too hot, not too cold, and plenty of sunshine! Plus, exercise will be good for you, Julianne. It'll fight some of that jet lag and help you to decompress at the same time."

Julianne agreed that some nature therapy would do her good, so she finally got on board. *Maybe I am ready to see the island,* she thought.

The first step of Bethany's plan was to hike along a trail that carved its way from the edge of her backyard through the island's rocky bluffs on the south shore up to the man-made beach on the flatter north shore of the island. From there, they would determine the next part of their plan. The final step was to head back to Eleanor's and look for her will.

Bethany changed out of her flip-flops and into her cross-trainers while Julianne prepared their water bottles next door. Bethany was feeling extremely energized when they started off, but after hiking a mere quarter mile up the trail, it was made crystal clear to her how out of shape she was. The more she tried to conceal her huffing and puffing to keep up with long-legged Julianne, the worst it got.

If Bethany were being honest, becoming friends (if that is what one would call it) with Eleanor had led to her sedentary lifestyle. She'd been so active when she lived in Southern California—always outdoors, surfing or hiking with Alex on the weekends and riding her bike everywhere. While she was fond of blaming her lack of exercise on the rainy Pacific Northwest weather, the truth was that her growing preoccupation with her next-door neighbor had led to more time sitting around, exchanging gossip, and indulging in the many sweet treats that she would bake for Eleanor on a regular basis. Put off by how breathless she was hiking from one side of the island to the other, she silently committed to get back into shape then and there.

When they finally reached the beach, Julianne took off her sneakers and socks. Bethany did the same, happy for the opportunity to bend over and catch her breath. She loved the sensation of her toes sinking into the warm, grainy sand. Bethany followed Julianne closer to the water's edge and was relieved when Julianne sat down on the packed sand.

"I would love to be out in that water right now," said Julianne.

"Mmm. Not me," replied Bethany before chugging down half her water bottle.

"Really? Not a water person?"

"I used to be. I practically grew up in the Pacific. I just can't tolerate the ice-cold temperatures anymore."

Julianne nodded. After a few moments, she pointed to the swimming area a few yards away. "My dad and I would go swimming over there all the time."

Bethany waited a beat before responding. "You were really close with your parents," Bethany said. She meant it as a question, but it came out more as an acknowledgment. Julianne simply nodded. Bethany studied her profile and noticed a tear roll down her cheek. Bethany had learned from Eleanor that her daughter and son-in-law had died in some sort of tragic accident years ago, but she had never elaborated on the details. Bethany could tell that the circumstances, whatever they were, caused a lot of pain, so she had never asked about it. She certainly wasn't going to ask now, even though she was eager to find out more.

Julianne and Bethany sat silently, side by side, staring at the waves lapping against the bronze shore. Bethany's thoughts drifted to the first time she came to this beach. Alex had just come home to their two-bedroom bungalow overlooking La Jolla beach and announced that he had made partner at his law firm.

The promotion, he said, required a move from his office in San Diego to Seattle.

Bethany was overjoyed and so proud of her husband, but she was simultaneously crushed to give up the cozy life they had built for themselves in the town where she grew up. She was willing to relocate for her husband, but she had one request: to stay near the water.

At first they rented a high-rise condo in downtown Seattle. For weeks, then months, Alex would go to work and Bethany would go out with Bessie, their real estate agent, in search of their new home. She feverishly scanned the top real estate websites looking for the perfect home with water views. She dragged Bessie to every town that hugged the shore of the Puget Sound to look at homes, many of which were substantially beyond their budget.

Bethany was discouraged and feeling tangible regret that she'd ever agreed to relocate in the first place. Then one evening, Bethany got a notification on her phone about an old redbrick farmhouse that had just gone into foreclosure and was on the market. The house—still priced at the tippy top of their budget—was on Jade Island. The forty-three photos attached to the listing took her breath away, a little more with each one. Bethany pulled up the map on her phone and typed in the address. Her heart sank. It was nearly two hours away and required a ferry ride from Port Forrester. There was no way Alex would be able to make that commute work with his schedule.

She tossed and turned in bed for hours that night until she finally emailed Bessie. The subject line read: *Let's Check Out This Jade Island House.*

As soon as Bethany stepped one foot onto Jade Island, she was home. The house sat high up, next to a forest of evergreens. From the front porch, you could see most of the low-lying island, and from the back windows you could see miles of restless sapphire water. Both the beach and the cute town were a short bike ride away. It was the closest she had felt to La Jolla since the move months ago.

She spent the entire return trip from the island to Seattle brainstorming how she would sell the island, the house, and its four-hour round-trip commute to her husband. She braced for a firm no when she showed the listing to him over dinner that night. But to her surprise, Alex seemed open to it. One of the senior partners at his firm had a house on Jade Island and had spoken very fondly of it. She was gobsmacked when he insisted they put in an offer the next day.

Bethany looked over at Julianne again, who seemed to be in a trance. She was not normally comfortable sitting in silence for so long, with only her thoughts to occupy her. She typically surrounded herself with noise, whether it was the TV, one of her true-crime podcasts, or the sound of Alex working from his home office. But sensing that this is what Julianne needed, she was able to dig deep and find comfort in the sounds of nature around them. At first she homed in on the waves. Then she started to notice the rustling of the leaves on the trees that swayed in the breeze behind them and the sounds of birds—gulls, warblers, and jays. She found it to be almost . . . *peaceful?*

Maybe, Bethany thought, *I should come down here more often.*

As the sun shifted high in the white sky and the day grew warmer, vacationers began to populate the beach and set up umbrellas around them. They had sat there nearly an hour when their quiet, tranquil setting finally eroded into the tourist hot spot that the beach is known for. Much to Bethany's relief, Julianne finally broke the silence.

"Antonio's is still around, right?" she asked. Antonio's was a little Italian restaurant down by the marina that shared a building with the ferry terminal.

"Sure is."

"I am craving their baked chicken parmesan, and I've been dreaming about their garlic butter breadsticks ever since I left."

"Well, let's go to Antonio's, then!" That was music to Bethany's ears. After a long hike and an even longer meditation on the beach, breakfast seemed a lifetime ago. She would start her fitness program tomorrow.

CHAPTER SEVEN

The last time Julianne dined at Antonio's was for her seventeenth birthday—the last one she would ever celebrate with her parents. The restaurant looked exactly like it did that afternoon, and Julianne couldn't tell if she was feeling comforted or anxious as memories from that afternoon started crawling back.

"Earth to Julianne," Bethany said, waving her hand back and forth in front of her face. "Do you want to dine inside or outside?" Julianne's wandering memories seemed to distract her from reality, like they had all morning.

"Oh, sorry. Let's eat outside. The weather's perfect," Julianne responded, shaking herself out of the past and reestablishing herself in the present.

After stepping inside to notify the hostess of their arrival, the new acquaintances made themselves comfortable on the patio. Julianne chose the same wooden picnic table, covered with the same red-and-white vinyl tablecloth, that she had sat at with her family so many times before. A server came over to take their drink order, and the two women were happy to discover that they were both ready to place their lunch orders as well.

"I'm glad you agreed to spend some time out of the

house today," Bethany said. "I know I said that it would be beneficial for you, but I think it's doing me a lot of good as well. I haven't been as physically active as I'd like since moving here."

"How long have you lived here?" Julianne asked. Just as she posed the question, the server brought their iced tea along with freshly baked breadsticks. Julianne couldn't resist, and she took a bite. The breadstick melted in her mouth, just as they always had when she was a kid. Even the iced tea flooded her senses with childhood memories. It was oddly reassuring to see that some things never changed.

"About five years," Bethany said, her mouth full of the warm, buttery breadstick. "We moved up here for my husband's work."

"What does your husband do?"

"Alex? He is a lawyer. His firm is in Seattle."

"Seattle? That's one heck of a commute," Julianne said before shoving another breadstick into her mouth.

"It is. Initially, we were going to have an apartment in the city, too. But it is amazing how much he has been able to work remotely from home. These days, he only goes into the city to meet with clients, and he'll couch surf at his coworkers' on occasion."

Julianne nodded politely, but much to her surprise, she found herself wanting to ask more questions. "Do you work?"

Bethany paused before answering. "I used to. Before we moved, I managed an auction house with my aunt. I really loved that job," she said dreamily. "But I never found anything here that really . . . suited me. So I have filled my days with other odds and ends. You know, interior decorating, volunteering—"

"Befriending elderly next-door neighbors and keeping them company?" Julianne added, to which Bethany cocked her head and smiled.

"Touché. But I absolutely adored your grandmother. She was a real hoot. And she had some great stories. I didn't realize it was her grand—well, I guess it was your great grandfather—who bought this island and built it from the ground up. That's quite a family legacy!"

"It is. Jade Island has always been special to us in that way. Now that she's gone, I'm not sure what's next. She and I never talked about what would happen if—er, *when*— she passed . . ." Julianne trailed off and took a deep breath. At that moment, the server came out carrying a tray with their lunch order.

"No need to worry about that this second," Bethany reassured her new friend. "Right now, let's just focus on these delicious creations! Mmm, baked ziti. Come. To. Mama!" She licked her lips and grabbed her utensils, preparing to destroy the cheese-covered bowl of pasta that was now in front of her.

As they were eating, a middle-aged woman with short gray hair cut into a bob approached the table from the sidewalk in front of the restaurant. Her stare concentrated on Julianne for a moment before asking, "Excuse me, are you Eleanor's granddaughter?"

"Yes, ma'am."

"I'm so sorry to hear about your grandmother," the woman said, dramatically clasping her hands together.

"Thank you, ma'am," Julianne said. *Wow, that news traveled quickly.*

"I'm Marie Hicks. I used to serve on the city council with Eleanor. I just can't believe she's gone. You know, one day we're talking about road improvements and then the next . . ." The woman stopped talking midsentence, apparently too choked up to continue. Normally, Julianne was comfortable consoling strangers—it was part of the territory that came with her job. But in this moment, she was at a loss as to how to respond to a stranger crying over *her* grandmother.

Bethany noticed and stepped in. "Yes, Mrs. Hicks. We are all going to miss her very much. Thank you for stopping by." Still choked up, Marie Hicks nodded dutifully and returned to where she'd come from.

"Thanks for . . . that," Julianne said.

"Anytime. Your family really are like local celebrities around here, huh?"

"Well, Grammy is . . . was. I guess a few folks on the island would dote over us from time to time when I was growing up. But I think her popularity grew after my parents died. Tragedy makes your stock rise." She raised her eyebrows and took a sip of iced tea.

"We don't have to talk about it," said Bethany.

"No, no, it's okay. I mean, it was ten years ago. Mom and Dad took a trip down to California to visit a friend. On their way back, Dad lost control of the car and . . . that was it. The weeks that followed were such a blur. I was a senior in high school at the time, and a few days after the funeral I got my acceptance letter to college. I just focused on getting to college and escaping the island and the memories of my parents after that."

"Did it work?"

"What? Running away?" Julianne asked. Bethany nodded.

"To some extent. It was difficult to talk to Grammy. She would speak about Mom and Dad as if they were still there in the house with her. For the first year or so, I avoided her phone calls and discouraged her from visiting me on campus. I was always *busy*," Julianne said, scrunching her fingers in the air to signify air quotes. "It wasn't until I started working at the hospital in my premed program and exposed to so many car accident victims and their families that I finally came to terms with what happened in my own life. Grammy and I grew closer after that. Well, as close as one can get to Eleanor Devereaux. Hmph."

This was only the third or fourth time Julianne had ever expressed these thoughts out loud to someone. Her therapist knew all of this, of course. Her best friend, Jenny, did, too. And she may or may not have divulged this information with a perfect stranger on the night of her white coat celebration. She had indulged in one too many mai tais (which, from that night forward, Jenny referred to as "Jules's truth serum"), resulting in an awkwardly over-personal sharing session with the cute bartender serving her. He was nice enough about it, but the cringe-worthy memory was enough to steer Julianne away from mai tais and oversharing with strangers ever again.

Bethany, Julianne realized, had quickly promoted herself from the stranger category to something more familiar and safe.

After lunch, Julianne and Bethany walked a few blocks toward the square. Julianne noticed that the flowers in the hanging baskets around town were Grammy's favorite shades of pink and orange. *She must have won that argument with the deputy mayor. No surprise there.* They walked up to Richard's bookshop, the Book Cellar. Through the storefront window, Julianne saw Richard sitting on a stool behind the cash register, speaking to a woman. From behind, the woman looked familiar.

Julianne and Bethany entered the shop. Richard lowered his glasses and gave them a wave. "Well, look who's here!" he exclaimed in his quiet demeanor. The woman at the counter turned around.

"Melissa?" Julianne said.

"Julianne!" Melissa replied. She trotted up to Julianne and gave her a hug. "Richard and I were just catching up. I am devastated to hear about your grandmother." Melissa tightened her squeeze around Julianne's shoulders.

"Wow, what are you doing here?" Julianne shook her head. "I'm sorry, that came out wrong. I just meant it's been a long time. I didn't expect to see you here."

"Do you remember Felipe and Margaret?" As Julianne nodded, Melissa continued, "I'm taking a couple of weeks off from adulting and staying at their house."

"Oh my gosh! Well, it is so good to see you," Julianne said.

"Yes, same here! Richard and I were just reminiscing about the summer that I stayed with you. Remember when we tried to dye our hair pink and it came out—"

"That rusty orange color? Please don't remind me! That was horrible." Julianne laughed as she put her head in her hands. She remembered that week well. It was early August. Her parents and grandmother had to leave suddenly for a few days. Melissa and her family were staying at the Santanas' at the time, and Melissa, who was a senior in high school, was asked to stay with an eleven-year-old Julianne. The girls rode bikes down to the beach almost every day and basked in the summer sun. Melissa introduced Julianne to Hawaiian Tropic tanning lotion and *Seventeen* magazine, while Julianne introduced Melissa to Neil Gaiman and Maya Angelou. They'd go to the square each evening to eat ice cream sundaes for dinner (their little secret) and pick out a rom-com to rent on DVD. Julianne had so much fun with Melissa that week that she didn't question the sudden departure of her parents and grandmother and, until she saw Melissa, hadn't thought about it since.

"I'm sorry, I'm being rude; Melissa, have you met Bethany? She and her husband live next door to my grandmother's house," Julianne said, gesturing toward Bethany.

Bethany stretched her hand out to shake Melissa's. "It is very nice to meet you," Bethany said.

"It's a pleasure," Melissa replied as she shook Bethany's hand. "Do you live in that adorable farmhouse?"

"That's home, alright." Bethany beamed.

Richard chimed in. "I was just telling Melissa that it would be nice to reconnect and share old tales. Why don't we all go out to dinner tonight? My treat."

"That would be lovely, Richard. I would really enjoy that," Melissa said. She looked at Julianne. "What do you say, Jules?"

Julianne looked at Richard and Bethany, who wore hopeful expressions. "Sure. Why not?" Julianne replied. Slowly but surely, her initial plans of lying low were being hijacked. But she wasn't sure if that was a bad thing anymore.

CHAPTER EIGHT

It was a well-known fact by locals and tourists alike that reservations were necessary at nearly all of Jade Island's fine-dining establishments several days in advance. What many tourists didn't know was that each restaurant kept one or two tables open on an "emergency" basis for locals—like Richard. When Melissa, Julianne, and Bethany walked out of the bookshop that afternoon, Richard called up his fishing buddy, David, who owned the Rose Cafe a few doors down. When he requested a table for four for that very same night, David simply replied, "No sweat, Rich!"

Melissa was the first one to arrive at the restaurant. After spending a majority of the afternoon planning her outfit for the evening, she finally settled on a white halter sundress and black canvas wedges that showed off her sun-kissed legs. She opted to diffuse her wavy strawberry blond hair to give off the appropriate sun-soaked beach vibes. After she finished applying her makeup, she looked herself up and down in the mirror. She hadn't looked this good in years. Since pre-kids. Possibly since pre-marriage. Hell, she wasn't sure she even looked this good on her first date with Chris. The bags that normally supported her heavy eyes were gone, and her skin was glowing. Even her lips looked smoother and plumper than usual. It was amazing what some new makeup and a few days without kids or work responsibilities could do for a woman.

Looking at herself in the mirror, her newly discovered self-confidence refreshed, Melissa decided to make a quick stop at Neptune's before dinner. Best-case scenario, she would see J.D. Worst-case scenario, she would walk away with some fresh coffee grounds for the morning.

Much to Melissa's dismay, Neptune's owner, a retired school principal, was the only one behind the counter when she arrived at the cafe. She wanted to ask about J.D., who had mentioned going out on the water after his shift, but she didn't. Instead, she made small talk with the owner as she picked out a bag of coffee and made her purchase. It seemed a shame that she wouldn't be able to flaunt this outfit in front of J.D. *Oh, well.* She looked this good once, she could probably pull herself together another time soon.

Even though she was a few minutes early, Melissa walked into the restaurant and looked around for some familiar faces. Nobody else had arrived yet. She walked back out to the sidewalk and pulled out her phone. No texts or calls from Fel and Margaret yet. She wasn't sure if that was a good sign or a bad sign. She hadn't FaceTimed with her kids, who were staying with their grandparents, since yesterday afternoon. It was the longest she had ever gone without talking to them.

Both her parents and in-laws were adamant that she take this solo trip so she could relax and shed her "mommy" responsibilities a bit. She was afraid she would be lonely without her kids, but she couldn't help but notice how much she was relishing this time alone as well as reclaiming her identity as something other than "Carson and Lily's mom."

Just as she was about to call Margaret to say good-night to her kids, Richard, Bethany, and Julianne strolled up the sidewalk. Everyone had dressed up as if it were a special occasion; Melissa was glad she wasn't the only one.

"Well, we all clean up nice, don't we?" Bethany said.

"Shall we?" Richard swung the restaurant door open and gestured to his guests to go inside. Everyone filed in. As soon as Richard walked through the doorway, a tall gentleman with a thick mustache standing near the kitchen waved his hand and started to make his way toward them. His breezy floral linen shirt made him look like he'd stepped out of the eighties version of *Magnum P.I.*

"Hey, Rich!" he said as he arrived at the hostess stand.

"David, my friend," Richard replied. The men shook hands.

As David was gathering menus, he held his hand up to his mouth and slyly whispered to Richard, "I saved you the best seat in the house." He gave a wink to the rest of the party. "Good evening, ladies."

"Good evening," they answered. He led them to a round table at the front of the restaurant. All of the floor-to-ceiling windows were open, welcoming the warm sea breeze into the dining area. David placed the menus on the table and pulled back a chair for Julianne.

"The Matriarch was our best patron. She will be dearly missed," he said. All the island residents had referred to Eleanor as "the Matriarch," but rarely in Julianne's presence. Or at least it had been a while.

Eleanor had earned the esteemed title as the eldest resident on the island and as a direct descendant of Jade Island's founding father, Grover Devereaux, the co-owner of the largest logging company in the Pacific Northwest. The commemorative plaque that stood outside the ferry terminal stated that he bought the island for its trees but took one step onto the island and fell in love. Instead of logging the island, he decided to incorporate the town of Jade Island. Eleanor's father and his brother, both professional loggers, wanted to inherit the island to grow their own businesses, which started a long family war. Instead, Grover skipped a generation and entrusted ownership of the land and his estate on the southern bluffs to his favorite granddaughter, Eleanor—or so urban legend would say. The rest is history.

After the server brought their drinks from the bar and they ordered their meals, Richard raised his glass to make a toast.

"I've seen a lot of changes on this island over the years. I've had friends leave for different reasons, but rarely do I see them return. Despite the reasons that brought you back here today, Julianne and Melissa, I, for one, am happy you have returned and that I can spend this time with you. This old fella doesn't take that for granted. Cheers."

They clinked glasses in the middle of the table and took a sip of their beverages.

"Grammy would have loved this, seeing us all together," Julianne said.

"She sure would have," Richard replied.

"I'm sorry if this is out of place, but have you made any arrangements for her yet?" Melissa asked. "I only ask because I know Fel and Margaret would want to pay their respects." Eleanor hadn't wanted a funeral in the traditional sense. She was open to a memorial service if that was what the town wanted. But over the last several years, she had made Julianne clearly aware that she wanted to be cremated and have her ashes spread under the large cedar tree in her yard, where her late husband's ashes had been spread many years before Julianne was born.

"That's a good question," said Julianne. "Grammy didn't want an over-the-top funeral, and from what I understand, she spelled out her wishes in her will."

Bethany interjected. "So once we find that, we'll know more." Julianne couldn't tell if she was referring to a collective "we" or a proverbial "we." She made note of Bethany's language, figuring she might have to discuss boundaries with Bethany later on. If the remainder of her time back on the island was anything like today, Bethany would probably wear her out.

"Time just got away from us today, but I'll look for it first thing tomorrow. I'm sure it is in Grammy's study," Julianne said.

Melissa opted to change the subject. "So, Richard tells me that you work for Doctors without Borders. That is fantastic!"

"It is a wonderful organization. I've been based in Iran since I was recruited earlier this year." Both Melissa and Bethany let out audible gasps.

"How did you get involved in that?" Melissa asked.

"I took a few humanitarian study-abroad trips to places like Haiti and Nicaragua when I was in my premed program at UDub. I have always wanted to travel the world and help the less fortunate."

"She almost didn't go. Isn't that right, Julianne?" Richard chimed in.

"Yes, that's true. But Grammy always encouraged me to do big things when given the chance."

"Traveling halfway across the globe to help others in need? I'd say that's a big thing, all right. That's really admirable," Bethany said. Julianne shrugged her shoulders and took a sip of wine. Attention and compliments always made her uncomfortable.

"Your grandmother was immensely proud of you for following your heart," Richard said, looking into Julianne's eyes to convey that truth.

"That's sweet of you to say, Richard. I always assumed she was, but I also knew she was heartbroken that I left here and never came back."

"You know what, kid? She knew why you left— No,

she knew why you *had* to leave. It was too hard on you to stay here."

Julianne had felt suffocated on the island after her parents' untimely death. Everywhere she went, she had vivid memories of the three of them, happy, together. And as the Matriarch's granddaughter on a tiny island where everyone knows everybody, the island residents didn't help her forget it, either. People were constantly sharing their own memories of her parents. They meant well, but it did her more harm than good. College was the perfect escape. And once Julianne got to college, she never looked back.

While Jenny and her therapist knew the whole truth, Julianne never openly discussed her feelings of suffocation with her grandmother. Eleanor was not one to speak openly about emotions, especially during hard times. During Julianne's first year at college, Eleanor drove to campus to visit Julianne a handful of times. Their visits were always nice, but never long. It was painfully obvious that half of their family was missing. Julianne would always make excuses as to why she couldn't come home for holidays or summer break, which Eleanor never questioned and always accepted. Whether it was an actual fact or hope at play, Julianne always had a gut feeling that Grammy knew the reasons she had to put Jade Island behind her.

After they finished their main courses, the server brought out cups and saucers for coffee to go with their dessert. Richard had ordered a raspberry cheesecake for the table to share.

"Melissa, you said you are on the island for a couple of weeks, right? What's the occasion?" Bethany asked.

Earlier, when Melissa was getting ready for dinner, she had toyed around with how much she would share with her old (and new) friends if asked. Melissa had been known to overshare in the past, but this group felt safe. Still, it wasn't often that she talked about her personal life. She was usually just busy living it.

"Not much of an occasion. More of an intervention you might say," she replied. The group looked at her with puzzled expressions, prompting her to say more. "Oh, where do I begin? For the past four years, I've been a full-time working single mother. I have two great kids, Carson and Lily. Between them, they are my world. Literally and figuratively. My in-laws and parents thought it would be a good idea if I went on a little bit of a vacation."

She had not signed up for the life of a single mother, but that was the hand she was dealt when Chris died. Lily had just been born, and they were getting into a new rhythm of being parents to a toddler and a newborn. Every morning, Chris would go out for a run while Melissa fed Lily and made Carson breakfast. One spring day, Chris kissed Melissa on the cheek and left the house in his running shoes like usual. But on that fateful morning, he never came back. Neighbors found him lying unresponsive on the sidewalk half a mile from their house. Chris, a young, physically fit father of two, had died of a sudden heart attack.

The room stood still. Bethany slid her napkin off her lap to dab under her eyes while Julianne said, "I had no idea, Mel. I'm so sorry."

Melissa was used to being on the receiving end of people's sympathy by now. For years, she felt the need to utter the words "Thank you" in response. But those words just added a layer of anger on top of the misery she was in. *Honestly, I'm not thankful for their sympathy. I don't want sympathy if it won't bring my husband back,* she used to think. Now, she accepted condolences with a shrug of the shoulders and a side tilt of the head. Someday, she might be able to do more.

"And you've just been going about, living your life for your kids for all this time?" Bethany asked. Melissa nodded. "You, my friend, are a very strong woman. Cheers to you." She symbolically lifted the empty wine glass that sat in front of her and tilted it toward Melissa.

"Listen, there are thousands of single parents out there doing what I do and more. I'm very fortunate that I have good support from the kids' grandparents. That's why I'm here having a lovely evening with you all." She took a sip of the dark roast coffee.

Richard had found peace in sitting back and listening to his guests share their stories throughout the evening. "I look around this table and I sense a lot of loss," he gently began.

Bethany interrupted. "Way to bring the mood down, Rich!" She was feeling the effects of the third glass of wine she had just finished.

"I know, I know, but please allow me to finish. Life is so complex. It gives us grueling losses and a fair share of heartache along the way. But it also gives us love. A love that we feel deep into our bones. My point is that if we don't have one, we truly don't know the other. So I'm grateful for it all. And I'm grateful for each of you and your willingness to join an old man for dinner this evening." Everyone at the table smiled in response.

"Hear, hear!" Melissa said and she raised her coffee cup. The others echoed her and did the same.

As Bethany lowered her cup, she saw her phone screen light up on the table. She picked it up. "It's just Alex," she announced. "He's letting me know that he got home. He had drinks with a client tonight."

"Well, let's get you all home so you can get some beauty sleep. I could really use some myself," Richard quipped as he mockingly pushed up on the wrinkles around his eyes.

Bethany, Julianne, and Melissa told Richard they were happy to walk back to their respective homes as a group. "It's a lovely evening for a walk under the stars!" Melissa exclaimed. But Richard wouldn't take no for an answer. He was adamant about his responsibility to drive them back and make sure they all got there safely. His stubborn tone sounded awfully familiar to Julianne.

Melissa was the first to be dropped off. She stepped up to the front porch and waved to everyone before blowing them a kiss, unlocking the door, and walking into the house. Once Richard saw the indoor lights turn on, he slowly backed out of the driveway and drove a short ways up the road to Eleanor's.

The car pulled up to the top of the driveway before Richard abruptly threw his foot on the brake, thrusting everyone forward in their seats. "What is that?" he asked as he squinted his eyes and peered through the windshield.

"What is what?" Julianne asked from the back seat. It was dark and she couldn't tell what he was looking at.

Richard put the car in park but left the engine running as he stepped out. "Stay here," he said. Julianne and Bethany sat in stunned silence as Richard gingerly walked up to the side of the house and stared at the windows of Eleanor's study before jogging back to the car.

"Call 911," he said as he quickly yet easily lowered himself back into the driver's seat. In one swift movement he closed the door and pressed the auto-lock button, securing everyone inside. He put the car in reverse and started backing down the driveway.

"What? Why?" Julianne asked.

"The windows are smashed. Someone has broken into the house." Richard's voice shook as he frantically backed out to the road, threw the gear into drive, and drove away from the house.

THE THIRD LETTER

February 1, 1975
Dear Mother,

    Well, the first few weeks of motherhood haven't been as smooth as I had hoped. Our baby boy arrived much earlier than anticipated. Ciarán Joseph Devereaux-Harris came into this world at just under five pounds. Since he was premature, he was immediately placed in an incubator to be monitored. For nineteen days I traveled back and forth to the hospital to spend time with him. He was released to go home just a few days ago, thankfully! Now, we are just adjusting to our new normal.

    Clark and I had started making plans to be married on Valentine's Day. It was going to be so romantic—on the beach at sunset. But due to the baby's early arrival, Clark and I were married by a priest in the hospital room just before the delivery. The nurses were our witnesses, and Clark raced across the street to a jeweler to purchase wedding bands. It wasn't the romantic wedding that I had dreamed about as a little girl—no wedding gown, veil, first dance, or three-tiered, decorated cake—but in the end, that all didn't matter. It was just important to me that we be married when we welcomed our baby boy. The labor went quickly—I'm just glad we found a priest in time!

    In addition to being born premature, Ciarán has colic and jaundice, which you can probably tell in the pictures I have included. He wants to be cuddled constantly and doesn't sleep well in his bassinet yet. Sleep is a rare commodity these days, which renders me pretty useless in all other aspects other than being a mother. Clark wants to help me with the baby, but he is also working two jobs to pay for our hospital bills. He even took on a second job and began sleeping on the couch downstairs so that the baby doesn't wake him.

None of this is how I imagined my initial journey into motherhood or being a newlywed. I am not too proud to admit that under the current circumstances, it feels very lonely and isolating. The baby books I read prepared me for this feeling, but I wasn't ready to also feel like I'm doing everything wrong. Every time Ciarán cries (which is very often), it is a painful reminder that I am not providing him with what he needs. And the sleep deprivation just worsens these feelings of ineptitude. Is it normal to feel this way? Your adoring daughter could use some reassurance.

I hope you are well and that your foundation work is sustaining you. If you ever get bored of the cold, rainy weather, you are always welcome here in sunny L.A.! Your grandson would love to meet you.

Love,
Ophelia

CHAPTER NINE

Wednesday, July 1
That didn't just happen, Julianne thought to herself. *It couldn't have happened.* Jade Island was notoriously safe and quiet, even with flocks of tourists each summer. Front doors were often unlocked, and windows were usually propped open around the clock in the summertime to welcome the warm and salty ocean breeze—at least they were before last night. But the neon yellow police tape that plastered the windows on the westerly side of the Matriarch's house—high on the hill and on display for the entire island to see—was about to change all that. Now, there were criminals on the island, casting fear and doubt that Jade Island was ever the safe place that everyone had thought it was.

Wrapped in Bethany's cotton terry bathrobe and with a freshly brewed cup of coffee in hand, Julianne slowly marched across the driveway from Bethany's front yard. She stopped to take in the damage in the daylight. As she peered through the shattered glass and police tape into the brightly lit study, she could tell this was an act of aggression. She noticed that many of Grammy's framed paintings had been torn off the walls. Shelves were thrown onto their sides. Furniture was slashed and pillows were gutted. Whoever did this, the goal wasn't just to find information; it was to cause mayhem and destruction.

But why? Who would do this? And why now? Was it just a coincidence that the house was burgled just days after Grammy's passing?

Bethany walked up behind Julianne. "It is unbelievable, isn't it?"

"It really is. I still can't believe what I'm seeing."

As Richard sped away from the house the previous night, Julianne called the police and described what they had come home to. The dispatch officer told Julianne to stay away from the house for the rest of the evening until they called back with an update. It wasn't until half past one in the morning that they called back. Richard, Julianne, Bethany, and Alex, who drove down to the square as soon as Bethany called, were sitting in Richard's one-bedroom apartment, located above his bookshop.

"We can't tell who was in the house, but we've begun our investigation. Please stay out of the house until you hear back from us," the officer said on the phone.

Alex overheard the officer and leaned closer to the phone. "Is it at least safe enough to go back to *our* house for the night? It's right next door."

The officer responded as Julianne turned on the phone's speaker. "We suspect this was a targeted offense. No other homes nearby should be in jeopardy."

"Whew, okay. Good," Alex said under his breath.

"Alex!" Bethany scolded him.

"I mean, that's good because Julianne can come back home with us. We will set the alarm system. We'll be safe."

The officer ignored this comment. "Julianne, we'll be in touch in the morning. Hopefully we'll have more answers for you then."

"Thank you, officer," Julianne replied, then ended the call.

"Are you sure you want to go back over there tonight? I can set you up in my bedroom. I'll take the couch," Richard said.

"Nonsense, Richard. We have a spare bedroom. Julianne will be fine with us," Bethany reassured him.

After contemplating her options, Julianne walked over to Richard and held his hands, just like she would with one of her patients. "I appreciate you so much for looking out for me. I think I'm going to stay at Bethany's tonight. We all need to get a good night's rest in our own beds as best we can."

Richard nodded solemnly. He stood up and embraced Julianne in a hug. The hug felt familiar to him, and then he realized she was the same petite size as Eleanor. It was like he was embracing his best friend again.

"Just stay away from the house," he said. Julianne furrowed her brow and tightened her lips to convey her understanding, then nodded at him. The three of them walked out the door and down the stairs. Richard looked out the window and watched as they piled into Alex's car and began the short drive back toward the scene of the crime.

As Julianne faced the broken windows and took another sip of coffee, she felt less steady than she had the night before. In her career, she was used to performing under high-stress situations with very little sleep. This was different. It had caught her off guard. The very little sleep she got during the night was going to work against her.

A car door slammed behind her, jolting her out of her thoughts.

"Ms. Devereaux?" she heard behind her. She turned around and saw two police officers climbing the driveway toward her and the house.

"Yes, that's me," she replied. *Grammy would have corrected them,* she thought, *and said "That's Doctor Devereaux to you."*

"Ms. Devereaux," the short and stout policeman repeated, "I'm Detective Roberts." He pointed over his shoulder to the taller and slimmer policeman. "That is Sergeant Gupta. We're the officials in charge of this investigation."

"Nice to meet you," Julianne replied. She turned toward Bethany. "This is my— Eleanor's next-door neighbor, Bethany." They politely exchanged greetings. The officer walked toward the broken windows in the study.

"As we told you last night, we believe this was a targeted attack. We don't have any major leads at the moment. This person did a good job of covering their tracks. But if you don't mind, we have some questions for you."

"I'd be surprised if you didn't," Julianne said.

Bethany suggested they go inside her house and talk over freshly brewed cups of coffee, which the tired officers enthusiastically accepted. A few minutes later, they were all settled in Bethany's living room, the detective and the sergeant in chairs, and Julianne and Bethany on the couch.

"I know we talked briefly about this last night, but do you have any idea who would want to break into your grandmother's home like this?" Detective Roberts began, as he took a small notepad out of his pocket.

"Not a clue," Julianne replied. "As I think you know, my grandmother is beloved on this island—"

"No doubt, Ms. Devereaux," replied the detective. "Just wanted to make sure." He scribbled something on his notepad. "Have you seen anything odd since you've been here?"

Julianne shook her head. "I have only been here for about forty-eight hours, Detective. But no, I have not."

"Did you tell anyone where you were going last night?" Detective Roberts continued.

"No, I haven't talked to anyone." Julianne paused. "Well, I texted my best friend, Jenny. She wanted to check in with me, but I told her I was going out to dinner with friends last night. She lives on the East Coast."

The detective turned toward Sergeant Gupta and whispered, "Let's get the friend's contact info later." He then turned and faced Julianne again. "Okay, last question for now. Was there anything of interest or of value in the room where the break-in occurred?"

Julianne thought there could be a number of things people would want. Money, bank account information, a deed to the island . . . the list probably went on. Unfortunately, she had no idea what her grandmother might have stored in her house or where anything was. If she had to choose a place to start looking, she would likely start in the study, but that was as far as she had gotten.

"Honestly, I don't know. I was going to start going through her files today to look for her will. Other than that, I just don't know." Julianne was starting to feel fatigued. The coffee hadn't kicked in yet.

"Okay, well, if you think of anything, please contact us. In the meantime, we'll continue our search of the property. You'll probably be good to come back this afternoon."

Sergeant Gupta, who had yet to string one sentence together, handed Julianne a business card as he rose out of his chair. "Call us if you think of anything else that might be helpful."

"What about the windows?" Bethany asked.

"I'd call around on the mainland to see if you can get those fixed as soon as possible. Insurance will take care of it, I'm sure," said the detective, before he and the sergeant showed themselves out of the house.

Julianne put her face in her hands. "What a mess," she said.

Bethany slid closer to Julianne and put her arms around her. "I know. What a weird, scary thing to have happened." Who in the world would rampage into Eleanor's house, destroy the study, and then just leave? It didn't make any sense. Unless someone was looking for something, something of value.

Julianne sat up. She took another sip of coffee, let out a heavy sigh, and pulled her cell phone out of her pocket. "Well, I guess I should shop around for a window installer."

CHAPTER TEN

News always traveled at lightning speed around the island, so it came as no surprise to Richard that there weren't many locals or tourists out and about in the square the day after the mysterious break-in at Eleanor's. Despite the perfect summer weather, which usually brought patrons out in droves, it was a quiet day at the Book Cellar. Richard knew that the frivolous spending moods of the locals had been dampened, and understandably so. He was preoccupied himself and could barely concentrate to do inventory, so he closed the bookshop early and drove over to Bethany's. As he got out of the car, he heard voices coming from the side of Bethany's house. He walked past a row of hardy magnolia trees and down a stone pathway that led to a screened-in porch. There, he found Julianne, Bethany, and Alex relaxing on the wicker patio furniture. Alex noticed Richard first.

"Hey, Richard! Come join us," Alex said enthusiastically as he waved Richard in.

Bethany turned around in her seat. "Hi, Richard! Would you like some iced tea? Just brewed it this morning."

"Iced tea on a hot day like this? Doesn't get much better than that," he replied. As Alex poured some tea into a glass and handed it to Richard, he couldn't help but notice how tragedy brought communities together. Seventy-two hours ago he only knew *of* Eleanor's neighbors, mostly through stories his confidant would share with him. Before Eleanor's death, he had met Bethany only a handful of times, usually when she shopped in his bookshop. He had run into Alex even less than that. Now, he was drinking iced tea in their backyard and chatting away like they were old friends.

He took a seat on the wicker sofa next to Julianne and studied her face. She was smiling politely, but he could tell her mind was elsewhere. He followed her gaze across the yard to Eleanor's house, where thick sheets of plywood had been nailed up.

"So, any news? Have you been back to the house today?" Richard asked, snapping Julianne back to reality.

"We were allowed back in the house a couple of hours ago, after they boarded up the windows. Grammy's study was demolished, top to bottom. They did a number on the place," Julianne said.

"Oddly, the rest of the house was virtually untouched. This wasn't some random B-and-E situation. The detective thinks this was done by someone who knows Eleanor," Bethany added.

"No leads on who did it yet, either. The police said it could take a couple days to a couple weeks to complete their investigation," Alex chimed in.

Richard felt chills travel up and down his spine. The topic of the police department's budget had come up for debate at one of last year's town council meetings. Serious crime was rarely reported on the island, and the council wouldn't approve an increase to the budget, leaving the island with a police squad that was about as useful as mall security guards—a JV squad at best. Richard had little faith in them with a situation *this* serious.

"What about the will? Eleanor's final wishes?" Richard asked.

"Unless she kept the will hidden in a different part of the house, anything of pertinence in that study is gone now," Alex said.

Julianne took a deep breath. Richard patted her back. "We'll find it," he said reassuringly.

"About that, actually," Bethany said. "We have a lead."

As Bethany and Julianne were surveying the damage at Eleanor's that afternoon, Alex called around to a few of his connections at various law offices around the state. His second phone call was to an old friend from law school who had become an estate lawyer in the Pacific Northwest. As luck would have it, she worked in the same office as Eleanor's estate attorney. After hearing Alex's story of what happened, she offered to prepare a copy of the will for Julianne to pick up.

"I'm going to pick it up tomorrow morning," Julianne said. Not only did a trip off the island sound idyllic, but so did the time alone. She wasn't used to being watched over and cared for so closely in a long time. Richard and Bethany had been terrific, but if she were being totally honest with them, they would learn that the constant attention was stifling. Julianne wasn't much of a people pleaser by nature— she'd certainly inherited her grandmother's genes in that regard— but there was an unfamiliar feeling in her gut that kept her from disappointing Richard and Bethany.

Before Bethany had a chance to make plans on her behalf, Julianne had already planned out her day. She would get up early, before her hosts even stirred in their bed, and go for a run up to the north shore and back before taking a quick shower and hopping on the first ferry off the island. She would sit in the back of the vessel with a cup of coffee and the book that she'd bought at the airport, which she had yet to crack open. After picking up the will, she would go to the pier and listen to a podcast or two as she enjoyed a refreshing lobster roll from one of the food trucks near the Port Forrester terminal. As she mentally put finishing touches on her daydream outing, Bethany interrupted her.

"I'm going to come with you. And I'm not taking no for an answer. In fact, I'll text Melissa. We can make a girls' getaway out of it!"

Julianne scrunched her nose. "Really, Bethany, that's very kind. But—"

"Nope. No buts!" Before Julianne could object any more, Bethany was texting Melissa—who had exchanged numbers with Bethany on the drive home the previous night—to invite her on the day trip, which would apparently include spa appointments and tastings at a boutique winery in Port Forrester.

Julianne looked helplessly at Alex as Bethany walked away to book their first appointment.

Alex looked back at Julianne apologetically. "Once Bethany gets excited about something, there is no stopping her. I guess it's been a while since she had girlfriends to go out with."

Julianne didn't want to seem ungrateful, and part of her felt bad for Bethany. She must have been so lonely, which explained why she had befriended her elderly neighbor, who had no shortage of stories to tell. Bethany's attachment to Julianne was starting to make sense to her.

Julianne sighed. She would set aside her introverted nature for one more day and dig deep within herself to match Bethany's enthusiasm.

Just then, Bethany bounced over and exclaimed, "Melissa's in! Manis and pedis are booked. This is going to be so much fun!"

"Yes," Julianne said, sighing to herself. Like sand through an hourglass, Julianne felt her relaxing dream day away from Jade Island slip through her fingers.

THE FOURTH LETTER

January 2, 1976
Dear Mother,

  Thank you very much for the Christmas care package. Ciarán was absolutely spoiled by all the presents you sent. As for me, your letter put me in great spirits. I'm so happy to know you are keeping busy. I am not surprised that you've been asked to serve as Jade Island's deputy mayor; the town council has sought your guidance off the record for years, so it makes sense that you will finally lead in an official capacity. You will fulfill that role beautifully.

  Clark and I have a few jobs hodgepodged together now so that we can make ends meet. He has moved into a management position with the construction company—the fastest any entry-level worker has been promoted! (I'm so proud of him.) I have begun nighttime shifts as a maintenance custodian after I put Ciarán to bed. I still find time to write during the day while he is sleeping. Speaking of Ciarán, we had hoped to throw a party to celebrate his first birthday, but with both of us working as much as we are, we have decided to postpone until next year. We'll make up for it when he turns two.

  Enclosed are a few copies of Ciarán's one-year portraits. I saved up to have them taken at Sears last week. I think he looks just like you. He certainly has your playful grin, which he notoriously flashes when he is up to no good, which seems like all the time! He's very cheeky and stubborn-headed (again, like his grandmother, if you don't mind me saying), and gives us a run for our money each and every day.

I know that our circumstances as mothers are quite different, but I have quickly learned how hard it is to be a parent, let alone a good one. I'm not saying I'm "good" at this by any means, but I am trying. Some days, we do okay, and other days . . . well, we don't. I guess I say all of this to express my gratitude for how you and Daddy raised me. I know it wasn't easy, especially since you did it on your own for the last several years. And the realization of how hard you worked to raise me makes me deeply desire your guidance in motherhood, too. If and when you are ever interested in communicating beyond letters, I hope you will. I miss you, and I would love for Ciarán to get to know his grandmother.

Love,
Ophelia

CHAPTER ELEVEN

Thursday, July 2

When Bethany texted with an invitation for an impromptu girls' getaway to Port Forrester, Melissa couldn't say yes fast enough. Melissa hadn't been on a girls' trip in forever, unless she counted the many field trips she'd co-chaperoned as part of the Mommy and Me classes she'd joined when Carson was a toddler. Her friendly outings these days mostly consisted of PTA meetings and fundraiser events for the kids' school. And she couldn't even remember the last time she went to a spa. It was well before the days of being a mom. She was giddy with excitement.

Bethany suggested that they meet at Neptune's at six thirty to caffeinate themselves for the day. Melissa agreed that was a great idea, omitting the fact that she was personally thrilled for another opportunity to see the cute barista who worked there.

As Melissa was about to leave for Neptune's the next day, she got a text message from Bethany:

> *Running late.* 😨 *Can you grab our drinks to go for us and meet us at the boat?*

Melissa replied:

> *Sure! No problem.* 🪽

This was good. She'd been nervous about facing J.D. in front of Julianne and Bethany. Now, she wouldn't have to worry. She checked her hair and makeup in the mirror one last time. She had thrown her hair up in a loose ponytail, revealing her long, slender neck. A few strands were meticulously styled to frame her face, to help her look as fresh and youthful as possible. She reapplied her lip gloss and whimsically strolled out the door.

By the time she arrived at the coffee shop about fifteen minutes later, she'd started to second-guess how good of an idea this actually was. Maybe he wasn't there, and she'd gotten her hopes up for nothing. Maybe he was there and was happily working side by side with his girlfriend or wife. Or, worse yet, maybe he was there and just had no interest in Melissa. All were likely scenarios in Melissa's mind.

She walked up the steps to the front door and peered through the glass pane. She immediately saw J.D., who was looking handsome as hell in a fitted black T-shirt. He was standing behind the counter, talking to an elderly man who was doctoring up his coffee at the barista station next to the counter. She took a deep breath and opened the door, the jingling bells announcing her arrival. As if it were in slow motion, Melissa saw J.D. break his gaze from the other customer and turn his head slightly in her direction. As soon as his baby-blue eyes locked on her, his face lit up with a smile. That smile told Melissa all she needed to know in the moment: there was no girlfriend behind that counter. Back in real time, he quickly finished up his conversation with the older man as Melissa walked up to the counter.

"Good morning," Melissa said. She had practiced her confident yet mildly sultry voice on the walk over.

"So, you came back to see me the other day," J.D. said. He had a playful twinkle in his eye.

"What?" Melissa asked.

"You stopped in two days ago . . ." J.D. started.

Melissa was clearly confused. "Bought some coffee grounds?"

"Wait, you saw me?" She was embarrassed. He had caught her.

"I was restocking in the back, and I heard your voice. By the time I came out front, you were already on your way out the door. I only caught a glimpse. You looked really good."

Blood raced to Melissa's cheeks. It had been years since a man had complimented the way she looked. She was never comfortable with direct compliments, but this felt different. *I guess wearing that dress did pay off,* she thought.

"I can't believe you were here," she muttered.

"I couldn't believe *you* were here and then left so fast. Had you stayed another minute longer, I might have had the chance to ask you out," J.D. said softly, as he shifted his gaze downward. *He is confidently assertive,* Melissa thought to herself. *But I don't hate that.*

"Oh, really? Well, there's always next time, I guess." Melissa shrugged, then grinned sheepishly.

"I suppose so," J.D. said. All of a sudden, he shifted his stance and became very businesslike. "So, what can I get you?"

Melissa's grin faded. "Three double-shot caramel soy-milk lattes," she said flatly. *Wait a minute. Didn't I just open the door for him to ask me out?* Maybe she had crossed signals or interpreted something wrong.

As he made the drinks, he asked, "So what kind of adventure requires double shots of espresso on this fine morning?" Melissa couldn't tell if he was just being friendly or if he was genuinely interested in her order.

"I'm going to the mainland today with some friends. One of them is meeting with a lawyer in town, so we're making a day out of it. We're catching the early ferry."

"Oh. Cool." His minimal response indicated no

genuine interest whatsoever.

"Oh"? "Cool"? That's it? Melissa was utterly confused by his reaction. One minute he was flirting with her, and the next he was barely saying anything.

He put a lid and a sleeve on each coffee cup as she got out her credit card to pay.

"So, is this next time?" J.D. asked.

"What?"

He'd caught her off guard. "You said 'there's always next time.' Is this a good time to ask you out?"

Melissa's look of confusion melted into a smile. She wasn't sure what was happening at that moment—he had definitely thrown her for a loop—but something made her want to say yes. "I suppose it is."

"Well then. Melissa . . ."

"Santana."

"Melissa *Santana*, will you go on a date with me?" J.D. asked.

"I thought you'd never ask," Melissa said. She reached across the counter and grabbed a pen. J.D. extended his right hand, suggesting that she write her number on his palm.

"I haven't done this since high school," Melissa said, as she tattooed ten digits on his palm.

"Did you write your phone number on a lot of guys' hands in high school, Melissa Santana?" J.D. asked. She could tell he was an experienced flirt. She would definitely need to keep an eye on that.

"If I told you now, then what would we talk about on our date?" With that, she grabbed the cardboard drink carrier and left. She decided to ignore the moment of awkwardness in their brief exchange and walked out feeling a boost of confidence and reassured that she could match his flirting with her own.

Melissa walked east through the square toward the

ferry terminal, balancing the drink carrier in one arm and reaching into her tote bag to pull out a pair of sunglasses with the other. As soon as she put on her glasses, she saw Bethany and Julianne standing in front of Antonio's. As she got within earshot, she called out, "Your coffee has arrived!"

"You are the best," Bethany said, as she gratefully accepted a cup. She took a long sip. "We stayed up way too late watching movies, didn't we?" She looked at Julianne.

"You stayed up. I fell asleep on the sofa," Julianne said. Her body had still not adjusted to this time zone.

"That's why you were able to get up so early and run!" exclaimed Bethany. "I am going to start working out again after things, you know, calm down." She didn't want to make Julianne feel guilty, so she added, "You know, Fourth of July on the island is always so busy!"

"Right," Melissa acknowledged. Melissa's form of working out was constantly chasing after two kids. That, in addition to her steadfast metabolism, kept her in pretty good shape.

They walked into the terminal building and checked the schedule on the giant screen inside the door. Their ferry had just arrived, loaded with passengers from the mainland. It would be boarding for its return leg in twenty minutes.

Bethany and Melissa stood near the entrance to the terminal, casually chatting away and sipping their drinks, while Julianne meandered inside and sat down in one of the rows of terminal seating. She watched the people who had just exited the ferry as they passed in front of her. She saw a man and a woman, about her age, each towing an oversized suitcase and a small child, a boy and a girl. They had probably rented a house on the island for the holiday week. She saw two middle-aged men walk by, holding hands. They both wore freshly pressed, bold-patterned shirts with crisp linen pants.

One of them had a leather satchel. They were probably a couple who had chosen Jade Island for a day trip in the Puget Sound. Behind them was a group of teenage girls, who were all on their phones as they bounced excitedly through the area. Julianne noticed a mix of bikini tops, halter tops, and tube tops paired with miniskirts and shorts. *They must have woken up hours before sunrise to get their hair and makeup styled this perfectly,* Julianne thought. Their biggest concern in life was probably getting the perfect shots for the 'Gram before heading back to their mundane teenage lives. *I hope you enjoy this time, ladies. Before you have to go to college and get a job. Before your family dies. Before you are faced with arduous tasks such as going on a hunt for a will so you can lay your Grammy to rest and move on with your life. Oh, to be young again.*

Out of the corner of her eye, she saw Bethany walk toward the restrooms. Melissa walked over and took a seat next to Julianne, interrupting her train of thought.

"Whatcha thinking about, Jules?" Melissa asked. She playfully knocked Julianne's shoulder with her own.

"Oh, nothing really."

"Are you looking forward to today?"

Julianne didn't respond right away, giving Melissa her answer.

"I know this must be a lot for you. If you need space or whatever it is that you need, just tell us. Okay?" Melissa's voice sounded so protective, just like Julianne's mom. Julianne's mom was perfect in her eyes. She wasn't like her friends' parents, who were either overbearing and too authoritative or absent and unreliable. Julianne had been blessed with a mom who was genuine and kind, always guiding her daughter with a gentle hand and encouraging her to follow her heart, no matter what. She found herself needing that guidance more and more as she got older.

Julianne squeezed Melissa's hand and said, "I'm glad you're here."

"Me, too," said Melissa.

CHAPTER TWELVE

Sam had only been on the island for a few minutes, and they were already head over heels. Jade Island reminded them of a small town not too far from where they grew up in the suburbs of Chicago—that is, if it were surrounded by sparkling water and majestic rocky forests. *And that fresh, floral yet salty aroma that hits you when you walk off the pier! Wow.* Sam finally understood how Jade Island captured visitors' hearts, just like it said on the tourism website.

The website also claimed that the sound of lapping tidal waves could be heard from almost every corner of the island (Sam made a mental note to test that out), and unless you were at the marina, where fishermen brought in their daily catches, you were almost always olfactorily enveloped in fresh pine, sandalwood, and citrusy magnolia. It seemed the tourism bureau was selling a vacation inside a meditation app, which Sam knew all too well.

Of course, this wasn't a vacation.

After a choppy forty-minute ride from the mainland, Sam staggered off the morning ferry and glanced at their watch: a quarter past eight. They hadn't gotten up this early in a long time, but they wanted to get a quick start on the day. Sam took out their phone to verify the address of the apartment they were renting during their stay. They were pleasantly surprised to find that everything on the island—including the rental—was within a short walking distance. The next step was to message the host:

> *Sorry to message you so early. I was able to take the first ferry over. Would it be possible to check in any earlier today?*

The host, Tina, replied back almost instantaneously:

> *Sure! Just follow Main Street through the center of town and turn left on Pine Street. The property is behind the pink house on the left - you can't miss it!*

It was about a fifteen-minute walk from the ferry terminal. Along the short walk, Sam was greeted cheerfully by at least a dozen folks, either on their morning dog walk or landscaping their impeccably manicured yards, which served as a wonderful accent to their midcentury Craftsman-style bungalows. Sam was enamored with the quaint downtown area, with its many restaurants, its shops, and a shaded park perfect for afternoon lounging. Not that they would have time for any of that. Even so, Jade Island was shaping up to be not too shabby for a work trip.

Sam approached the flamingo-pink house. The owner was right—it was definitely difficult to miss. The rental unit was described as a one-bedroom apartment above the garage in the backyard. Sam walked up the driveway toward said garage when a woman greeted them from the backyard.

"Hello!" she said with cheerful exuberance. "You must be Sam."

"Hi!" Sam said, trying to match the woman's energy as they extended their hand. "Nice to meet you."

"Likewise! I'm Tina." The middle-aged woman reached out and gave a firm handshake. Through her sunglasses, she studied her guest's freckled face and purple pixie cut for a moment before gesturing toward the stairs on the side of the garage. "After you."

Sam got to the stairs first, waited for Tina to catch up, and then followed their host up the stairs and watched her punch the entry code on the panel above the door handle. The door swung open, and Sam followed her inside. Tina began her "welcome spiel," as she called it, as Sam placed their bags inside the door and took in the eclectic but warm living space. The apartment was an open floor plan filled with mix-and-matched furniture: a worn brown leather couch, a large pink suede armchair, and a retro kitchen table set with mustard yellow chairs. The walls were lined with meticulously organized wooden bookshelves that held both novels and vinyl records. Tina even had a three-wick candle burning on the coffee table in the sitting area. Sam immediately felt good vibes about this place and understood why it had a five-star rating.

"The bed, bath, and laundry are through that door," Tina said as she pointed to the door in the back between two of the bookshelves. She picked up a three-ring binder from the kitchen table to show Sam. "And all the information that you need about utilities, Wi-Fi, trash, getting around town, and that sort of stuff can be found in this manual."

"This is perfect, Tina. Thank you."

"And you are staying two weeks. Is that correct?"

"That's the plan," Sam confirmed. Actually, Sam didn't have a plan. They had hope and an estimate that the job would be done in two weeks' time. If not, they would make alternative arrangements—they were used to being flexible at a moment's notice.

"Wonderful. Well, I'll leave you to unpack. Text me if you need anything."

"Will do," Sam said, closing the door behind their host.

They reached into their pockets to pull out their

wallet and cell phone. Seeing that they had missed a phone call from their sister, Sam thought, *She probably saw my post about taking the ferry.* They would call her back later.

Sam grabbed a laptop out of their bag, along with the Diet Coke they'd bought at the ferry terminal earlier that morning, and sat down at the kitchen table. The mustard yellow chair wobbled a bit beneath them, suggesting that these were original furniture pieces, which Sam appreciated much more than if they were new and made to look vintage.

They opened their email and saw no new messages. Which meant no potential new clients. Sam knew that this business ebbed and flowed and that starting up a new business took time, but it still made them nervous. While flexibility was one of Sam's strong suits, patience was not. They were excited when the client on Jade Island seemed to appear out of thin air, so maybe future clients would, too. Speaking of, they needed to send an email to let the client know that they had successfully arrived on the island.

After Sam clicked the Send button, they took a deep sigh of relief and gently closed the laptop. After they finished their soda and the half-eaten granola bar in their bag, they'd go back to the park surrounded by all the shops. Traveling to new places was one of the best aspects of their line of work, but the process of arriving, checking in, and meeting new people always brought on elevated levels of anxiety. On this occasion, their arrival went about as smoothly as could be expected. They just hoped that the rest of their time on the island would follow suit.

CHAPTER THIRTEEN

From the top deck of the ferry, Julianne stared off into the distance and watched Port Forrester get smaller and smaller as they crossed the sound. If Julianne was being honest with herself, all things considered, she'd enjoyed the outing more than she thought she would. Yes, Bethany's self-imposed invitation and her hijacking of her ideal trip was off-putting at first. But after succumbing to the fact of the matter, Julianne was determined to have an adequate time at the very least. As the day unfolded, she began to actually take pleasure in the company that surrounded her. She might even say that she'd felt herself developing some sort of bond with Bethany and Melissa. Other than Jenny, who'd she met when they were assigned as roommates freshman year, it took quite a lot for people to wedge their way into Julianne's life—at least long term.

She thought back to their first encounter and how Bethany's big energy almost knocked Julianne backward when she'd opened her grandmother's front door. It was quite different from her own subdued personality and definitely took some getting used to, like an acquired taste for a rich espresso when all you ever drank was herbal tea. But she also noticed that Bethany was selfless at her core and spent a bulk of her energy on giving to others. For instance, Julianne had practically wanted for nothing since Bethany entered her life. Bethany took care of anything that Julianne wanted and even some things she didn't necessarily want but probably needed, like the girls' trip. And while all the attention had made Julianne uncomfortable at first, she was starting to get used to it.

While walking around downtown Port Forrester with her new companions, Julianne was reminded of the good times she'd shared with Jenny when they were in college. Every year, on each of their birthdays, they would treat each other to mani-pedis followed by a lavish dinner at their favorite sushi bar near campus and a movie. They'd fill the day with talk about all the things seemingly trivial and inconsequential that preoccupied them, such as the best movies they had seen, details about the latest dates they'd gone on, gossip about their least favorite professors, and so on and so on. They would be completely present with each other on those birthday celebrations, just enjoying the day together. When they graduated, Julianne moved on to medical school, while Jenny followed her boyfriend (now, husband) across the country to Massachusetts. After she moved, that was it, the end of their birthday celebrations. It had been a long time since Julianne had thought about those days. She hadn't realized just how much they still meant to her until spending the day with Bethany and Melissa.

Yet as much as she'd enjoyed their company, the introvert within Julianne was desperate for some quiet time alone to recharge her batteries when the ferry finally returned to the island. Bethany had arranged for Alex to meet them outside the terminal to drive them back home. When they got to the car, Julianne excused herself from the group to "check in with Richard" instead. The tranquility of the bookshop and Richard's calming presence was calling her name.

As the sun began to touch the tall emerald evergreens that bordered the western side of the island, a cool breeze swept through the town. Julianne picked up her pace as she neared the Book Cellar, then swung open the door to what appeared to be an empty shop. Richard was missing from the stool where he normally perched himself during the day. "Hello?" she called out.

"Hello!" a faint voice called from the back, where Richard housed all of the used books. A moment later, Richard walked to the front of the shop, dusting his hands off. "Welcome back," he said as he took his place on his stool.

"Thanks," Julianne said. She put down the shopping bags that she had accumulated throughout the day and leaned on the counter.

"So. How did it go?" he asked.

"Do you want the good news first or the bad news?"

"Always bad first," he said, as if it were obvious.

"The lawyers did not have the will."

Richard squinted his eyes. "I don't understand."

"By the time we got to the office around noon, the receptionist said that someone else had already picked up the document," Julianne said exasperatedly.

"Who was it? Did they give a name?"

"I don't know. They wouldn't give me that information."

"And they wouldn't give you another copy?"

Julianne shook her head. "Other than my license, I had no proof on me that I'm Eleanor's next of kin. Considering that they had already given a copy to someone who claimed to be her relative, I think they were spooked and didn't want to make the same mistake twice before investigating." Julianne slouched.

Richard looked cross. "This doesn't make a lot of sense, does it?"

"Zero sense. I mean, who else could it be? And what would they want with it?"

"Hey, Richard?" somebody said from behind Julianne. Julianne jumped. She hadn't expected anyone else to be in the bookshop. Clearly, she had become easily startled and jumpy in the past forty-eight hours.

"I'm so sorry, I didn't mean to scare you," Sam said as they approached the counter.

Julianne took a step backward, then crossed her arms in front of her chest to calm herself. "No worries," she replied to the stranger.

"Ah, Sam. This is Julianne," Richard said as he introduced the two of them. "Julianne, this is Sam. They are, um, a writer working on the island for the summer." Julianne extended her hand, then shook Sam's.

"Nice to meet you, Julianne," Sam said softly. It looked like Julianne had had a rough day, and they didn't want to add to her discomfort.

"Likewise," Julianne replied. "You are a writer? What do you write?"

"A little bit of everything," Sam replied, glancing up at Richard, "but mostly freelance copywriting for advertising companies."

"Yes, Sam popped into the shop, and we got to talking. We're going to grab some dinner as soon as I close up. Would you like to join us?" Richard asked.

"Thanks for the invite, Richard, but it's been a long day. I'm going to take a rain check." Julianne bent down to pick up her bags. The long day was quickly catching up with her, and she suddenly felt the desire to lie down and rest.

Richard pulled a set of car keys out of his pocket and held them out in his palm for Julianne. "Here, take the car. I'm not going to have you carrying all those bags back up to the house. It's parked in the alley round back."

Normally, Julianne would argue and find the walk

back to be an endurance challenge, but she was exhausted in every way possible. She simply smiled in appreciation as she slid her finger through the key ring.

"Wait! What was the good news?" Richard asked as he let go of the keys.

Julianne sighed and gave a weak smile. "It was a really nice day with Bethany and Melissa. I haven't had a day like that in a long time."

Richard slowly bowed his head. "Good. You deserve more days like that." Julianne paused as she pondered that statement before taking a step toward the front door.

"Sam, it was nice to meet you. Richard, I'll call you tomorrow." Julianne swung the door open and stepped out.

When the door shut behind her, Richard turned in his stool and looked at Sam. "Did you catch all of that?" he asked.

"I did. Looks like I have my work cut out for me," Sam replied.

"I'm afraid you do," Richard said as he went back to work.

CHAPTER FOURTEEN

Melissa didn't admit anything to Julianne or Bethany, but she had butterflies in her stomach all day. Ever since she wrote her phone number on J.D.'s hand, she had become mildly obsessed over her phone, even knowing, deep down, that she was acting totally out of character. In between each conversation with the girls, her mind strayed. *Would he text right away, or was he one of those guys who waited a few days to avoid looking eager?* Melissa was glad that her phone had remained call-less while on the mainland. But now that she was back on the island, she hoped that he would call sooner rather than later, or her next trip to Neptune's might be awkward.

While the butterflies excited her, she also felt a twinge of turmoil. The last time she felt excited for a date was with Chris when they'd first started officially dating. They had lost touch when he went off to college. Then, to celebrate one New Year's Eve during her junior year of college, Melissa flew cross-country to go out with high school friends in New York City, where Chris lived at the time. As fate would have it, they ended up at the same popular nightclub on the Lower East Side, arriving just minutes apart. They flung into each other's arms as soon as they locked eyes on the dance floor. After dancing all night long and sharing a passionate kiss—

their first kiss—at midnight, they knew they had reconnected for good.

Melissa and Chris had made so many memories all over the island since they were practically kids. The sights and smells of the island *were* him. How on earth was she supposed to go on a date with another man and not think about her husband? Was she making a mistake?

As she mulled over these questions, an unknown phone number appeared on her screen. Panic momentarily set in. That must be J.D. She thought that most guys texted before calling these days, but apparently he was old-school. *He does appear to be in his midforties, so that tracks,* she thought.

She answered the phone hesitantly. "Hello?"

"Hello, Melissa Santana," said a low baritone voice. It was definitely J.D. They exchanged pleasantries and asked each other about their day. Then he asked the question she had been both hoping for and dreading.

"So, how about that date?"

"Yes. Um, about that . . ." She still didn't know what she was going to say.

He interrupted her thoughts. "Don't tell me you've changed your mind, darlin'."

There he goes again, Mr. Prince Charming, Melissa thought. "No, not at all. It's just, well, I feel the need to be up-front and honest with you about something," Melissa said.

"Okay . . ." J.D.'s tone shifted from charming to concern.

"I'm just going to come out and say it." She paused. "I'm a widow." Silence on the other end of the phone compelled Melissa to continue. "My husband—well, late husband—and I met on this island when we were kids, and he's still very much a part of Jade Island for me."

The other end of the line was still silent. *He probably hung up and never wants to see me again,* Melissa told herself.

"I understand." J.D.'s voice sounded comforting. "If you aren't ready, then we don't have to— "

"No, no. I want to go out with you. I actually want to more than I thought I would, honestly. It's just that there are some places around here that I just can't . . ." Melissa trailed off.

"Say no more, Melissa," J.D. said. His voice was calming. "You call the shots on this date. All right?"

Melissa was relieved. She recommended that they meet at Antonio's for dinner (it was Chris's least favorite restaurant on the island after getting food poisoning there as a kid), followed by an evening stroll up to the north shore and back. J.D. enthusiastically agreed.

"So, when should I pick you up?" J.D. said.

"Tonight? You want to go out tonight?" Melissa asked.

"Why wait, darlin'?" J.D. retorted.

"I mean, there's a chance we won't get a table at Antonio's. It is really busy this time of year."

"Let me worry about that."

"Okay. Well, how about I meet you there. Say, around seven thirty?"

"It's a date," he said.

Melissa hung up the phone and looked at her watch. She had an hour before she had to leave the house. To calm her first-date jitters, she decided to FaceTime with her kids. She called Margaret, who picked up on the first ring. Seeing her kids after a couple of days made her heart sing. When her parents and her in-laws first suggested she take this trip, she'd protested. She couldn't imagine being away from her kids for so long. After multiple conversations with Margaret and her own mother, she was finally persuaded to believe that this was healthy for them in the long run. It was healthy for *her*.

She caught Margaret, Carson, and Lily in the middle of a movie before bedtime.

"We're watching Elsa, Mommy!" Lily exclaimed as she popped popcorn into her red Kool-Aid-stained mouth. She could only imagine how much sugar her babies were consuming in her absence. Fel and Margaret adored their grandchildren and often bent to their will, which was a far departure from how they'd parented Chris and his brother. *But that was a grandparents' job, right?*

"It's called *Frozen*, Lily," Carson lovingly corrected his little sister.

Melissa told them how much she missed and loved them, but she could tell they were more interested in the movie at that point. Carson and Lily returned to watching the movie—a movie they had watched nearly two dozen times—leaving Margaret with the phone.

"Melissa, my dear, Felipe and I were talking earlier today. We thought it would be a fun day trip to bring the kids over to the island to watch the fireworks this weekend. What do you think?"

"Yes! Absolutely!" Melissa's grin grew from ear to ear.

"Splendid. I'll send Felipe to the supermarket tomorrow to pick up the food for a cookout," Margaret said. It had taken Melissa a while to get used to Margaret's commandeering nature, especially when it came to food and family gatherings. When Chris and Melissa first got engaged, she'd dreamed of hosting big family gatherings, where she would make a big spread for everyone. But every time she invited Fel and Margaret over, Margaret would take over. For years, this caused tension between the new bride, who wanted to impress her new in-laws and show off her homemaking skills, and her mother-in-law. Melissa would set the menu and then Margaret would call the day before, essentially scrap Melissa's plans, and set an entirely new menu. After all the guests had left—whether it was a summer cookout or a birthday dinner— Melissa would retreat to their bedroom and cry. Chris would come in and console her every time. "Don't take offense. My *abuelita* did the same thing to her. Consider it a rite of passage," he'd say. Chris would always convince Melissa to shake it off until the next family gathering, to which Melissa would vow to speak up for herself and take the reins the next time. But she never found the strength to speak up to Margaret, and the cycle continued every time she invited Margaret and Fel over. That cycle eventually ended when Chris died; from that day forward, Melissa happily let Margaret steer the ship.

Melissa blew kisses to her kids, wished them sweet dreams, and hung up. She looked at the clock and realized she had about ten minutes to get ready before she had to leave the house in order to meet J.D. in time.

She stepped out of the jeans and white T-shirt that he'd seen her wearing that morning at Neptune's and ripped off the tags on the pink cotton maxi dress she'd bought in Port Forrester earlier that afternoon before stepping into it. She slipped her freshly manicured toes into her white Converse and put on a pair of gold dangling earrings. She finally checked herself out in the hallway mirror one last time before she grabbed her black leather clutch. "It'll do," she said to her reflection.

She reached for her keys in her purse as she pulled the oversized front door toward her. Distracted, she walked across the threshold and nearly ran into somebody as they were about to knock on the door.

"Oh!" she squealed as she jumped backward. She blinked her eyes a few times to make sure she wasn't hallucinating.

In front of her stood J.D.

On Fel and Margaret's front porch.

Holding a bouquet of bright yellow and orange Asiatic lilies.

CHAPTER FIFTEEN

"J.D.!" Melissa exclaimed. "What are you doing here?"

"I wanted to surprise you," J.D. replied. He had accomplished his mission.

"Yes, yes, this is a surprise," Melissa sputtered. "How did you know where I was?" She wanted to sound curious, but her tone came off as uneasy at best.

"Let's just say I'm resourceful," he said. He pushed his hand forward, presenting the large bouquet of flowers. "For you."

Melissa took the flowers from him—her *favorite* flowers—and inhaled their sweet aroma. "They are lovely," she admitted. The sweet gesture would be enchanting if they were anything other than her favorite flower. She didn't want to ask how he knew. It might have been a pure coincidence, but if it wasn't, she didn't want to know. She thought about inviting J.D. into the house while she put the flowers in a vase, but something didn't feel right about welcoming her date into her in-laws' home. Instead, she leaned in and carefully placed the bouquet on the entryway table before closing and locking the door behind her.

"Were you afraid I would get lost on my way to Antonio's?" Melissa joked, trying to ease the tension she was feeling.

"Well, there has been a slight change of plans. Hence, the reason I decided to meet you here instead of at the restaurant."

"Oh, really? May I ask what the new plans are?"

"You may," he responded with his boyish charm. "I have something a little more personal planned for us. What would you say to a picnic down at the marina?"

"Oh. Sure, I love picnics." While the idea of a picnic at sunset seemed lovely, the marina didn't necessarily sound romantic to Melissa. She eyed him carefully, still shocked by him showing up at her in-laws'. She decided to give him the benefit of the doubt and chalk up his detective work and sudden change in plans to being romantically sweet. Instead of holding back, she followed his lead down the driveway toward the quiet street.

Their conversation picked up as they started walking. They filled the time talking about the marine life they had spotted around the island (orcas, seals, and dolphins), childhood pets (Melissa had terriers and J.D. had an infinity for rats), and the formative movies they watched dozens of times growing up (*Clueless* and *Dead Poets Society* for Melissa, *Fight Club* and *Trainspotting* for J.D.). Melissa was surprised by how natural their conversation flowed as they winded up and down streets, along the gravel footpaths that zigzagged across the park in the center of the square, past the ferry terminal and all the way down to the marina on the north end.

As he talked, Melissa inspected her date closely. He was wearing a pair of boot-cut black Levi's and a freshly laundered off-white Henley. He had rolled up the sleeves just enough that some of his tattoos were visible on his forearms. He had recently showered but not shaved his stubble-lined cheeks; his hair was freshly tousled, and whenever Melissa was downwind of him, she caught an unmistakable whiff of

Irish Spring. He didn't appear to have put a lot of effort into his look. He didn't have to. He was naturally handsome as far as she was concerned.

When they got to the marina, J.D. took Melissa's hand in his and led her behind the bait and tackle shop to the end of one of the docks. At first Melissa was taken aback by how nicely her fingers interlocked with his. But after a second, she began to grow nervous. *What if a friend of Fel and Margaret sees us? What might they say?* As her anxious mind wandered, she slowly untangled her fingers from his just as they came to a stop in front of a forty-foot daysailer.

"This is *your* boat?" Melissa asked.

"Well, not really. It's a friend's," J.D. admitted. "But he lets me use it from time to time. On special occasions."

As they got closer, Melissa noticed a picnic basket and some blankets spread out on the deck. *Oh, my. This guy really knows how to charm a gal,* Melissa thought. He took a short leap onto the boat and reached for her hand.

"My lady?" His smile just glistened.

Melissa hesitated. "Where are we going?" she asked cautiously.

"Oh, nowhere. This is it." His smile began to fade. "Are you disappointed?"

"No, this is perfect." A relieved Melissa extended her hand and allowed him to assist her onto the vessel. The water was calm, and the boat gently bobbed up and down.

She sat down on the blankets and draped the hem of her dress around her. He sat down next to her. As their knees gently knocked together, a spark of electricity raced through Melissa's body. She watched as he opened a bottle of wine and filled two glasses. Melissa took one and looked at J.D.'s face, lit up by the glistening sunlight reflecting off the water.

"To you," he said.

"Me?"

"Yeah, you. You didn't have to go on this date. But

I'm sure as hell happy you did."

"You know what? I think I'm happy I did, too," Melissa admitted.

Their conversation easily flowed over one glass of wine, then another. At one point, he emptied the contents of the basket onto the blanket, including napkins, utensils, a charcuterie board that he had bought at the market, and, the grand finale, a pair of chocolate pudding cups.

"Chocolate pudding?" Melissa tried not to sound judgmental, but she couldn't help herself. He laughed and boyishly shrugged his shoulders.

"I wanted to share one of my favorite desserts with you," he said. "That, and I went all out for the charcuterie board and wine. Pudding, it turns out, is pretty economical."

Melissa raised her eyebrows with feigned surprise.

"So, is this the point of the date where we talk about our pasts and share our life stories with each other?" she asked. She felt ahead of the game because she had already revealed a huge part of her past before the date.

"Well, whaddaya want to know?" he said confidently.

"Let's start with where you grew up."

"California."

"Okay. That's cool. Is your family still there?"

"Nah," J.D. replied coolly before taking another swig of wine. Melissa got the sense that the topic of family might be off-limits.

"Where does the name J.D. come from? Are they initials for anything in particular?"

"I'm named after my granddad, actually. J.D. is just a nickname, I guess," he said.

"Really? I love family names that are passed down like that." She thought back to the many times she and Chris discussed baby names before both their children were born. If the baby was a boy, she wanted to name him Christian James, after him, but Chris pushed back. He wanted his son to have an original name. They decided on Carson Javier instead, settling on her father-in-law's middle name and the same initials. "So, what brought you to Jade Island of all places?" Melissa asked.

"What is this, the Spanish Inquisition?" J.D. laughed at his own question as Melissa shifted backward with a frown—his joke had obviously come off as more accusatory than he had planned. "Sorry," he said. "So back to your question. I guess I just wanted a change of scenery. I'd heard so many great things about this part of the country. So I quit both my jobs, packed my bags, and took the 101 up the coast until I arrived here." J.D. was turning out to be more of a free spirit than Melissa had conjured up in her mind.

"That must have been a beautiful road trip." Melissa sighed.

"Taking my bike on the road is my favorite place to be. There are some beautiful scenic cliffs that overlook the ocean out there. Just absolutely gorgeous." J.D. seemed to drift away to another place momentarily before Melissa asked him another question.

"Were you a barista before?"

J.D. chuckled. "Oh, no, no, no. I had a bunch of different jobs here and there. You know, construction, handyman . . . I worked as a waiter once. I'm a quick learner," he said before taking another swig of wine. "What about you?"

Melissa had debated about how much information to disclose on a first date. He already knew about Chris and where she was staying, so he likely knew her in-laws owned the house. She decided to play it safe and begin with her childhood background.

"I grew up in Tacoma. Went to UDub for college, then moved to New York for a while before getting married." She kept it short and sweet, hoping to move the conversation along to something else.

"And now?" J.D. asked.

"And now . . . ?" Melissa stalled, pretending she was seeking clarification. Was she ready to reveal that she's a mom to two young kids? That she knows all the words to all the Wiggles' songs and every episode of *Peppa Pig*?

"What does your life look like now?" J.D. clarified.

"Well, I'm back in Tacoma now. I work for my dad," Melissa started. "And . . ." She inhaled. "I'm a mom." She decided to rip off the bandage and come out with it.

"Oh, really? That's . . . awesome," J.D. said lightly. One of the things Melissa always feared about dating again was the possibility that she wouldn't find a guy who wasn't scared off by dating a mom. Melissa gave him the CliffsNotes version of Carson and Lily. As she talked about them, she couldn't help noticing that he was zoned in on every word she said. She felt relieved—it was truly the best-case scenario. Looking back, he had been paying careful attention to her the whole night. *Is this guy for real?* she wondered to herself.

The evening flew by. Before they knew it, the bottle of wine was empty and the sun had disappeared behind the purple horizon. It had been a long day, so it was probably best to call it a night and walk back to the house before the purple sky turned pitch black. If she waited too long and let herself be even further ensorcelled by this man, she might never get off this boat. She started to tidy up the dishes on the blanket around them before J.D. touched her arm to stop her. "Whoa, whoa, whoa. What are you doing?"

"It's getting late. I should get going," she said.

He brushed a strand of hair away from her face and tucked it behind her ear. "I was hoping we could stay a little longer. There's supposed to be a pretty amazing meteor shower tonight." His twinkling blue eyes gazed into hers.

Every fiber of her being but one was telling her to stay. She wanted to feel another jolt of electricity like the one she'd felt before. If his knee held that much power, she could only imagine how those pouty lips would make her feel. She was about to bend to her temptation. The word *Sure* was on the tip of her tongue when her phone buzzed in her purse. She glanced down at her bag and noticed a text message from Margaret. It was a photo of her kids holding each other as they slept on the couch in the glow of the television. Immediately, J.D.'s lust spell was broken. Her senses came back to her, and she knew what she had to do.

"I would love to stay later, but I'm getting tired. I hope you don't mind," Melissa said.

"No, no. Not a problem." J.D. said as he started to get up. "At least let me walk you home."

Melissa contemplated turning down his offer, but if she was honest with herself, she wasn't ready to say good-night yet. "Only if you insist," she said.

"Oh, I definitely insist."

The stroll back to Fel and Margaret's was less talkative than their earlier walk. The evening orchestra of crickets, frogs, and the occasional barking dog filled the void that they were too nervous not to fill themselves earlier. As they walked, Melissa hoped that J.D. wasn't getting the wrong message about her ending their date early. *Should I admit why I'm ending the date?* she thought to herself. *Or should I leave it alone? He's a pretty smart guy. He probably gets it.* The silence between them felt natural anyway. *Why ruin a nice moment?*

As they approached the driveway, J.D. reached for Melissa's hand. He entangled his fingers with hers and squeezed gently. "We got you back before you turned into a pumpkin," he joked.

"I don't think Cinderella turns into a pumpkin in that story," she said.

"Who said you are Cinderella?" J.D. retorted with a goofy grin on his face. She shot him a look and playfully slapped him on the arm with the hand he wasn't holding captive. His joke broke any of the leftover tension from before.

When they stepped onto the front porch, Melissa reached her arms around J.D.'s neck and stood on her tiptoes as she pulled him in for a hug. He wrapped his arms around her waist and held tightly. He buried his nose into her neck and inhaled deeply. Melissa resisted letting go, fearful of what he might expect when she leaned away. The thought of having her first kiss since Chris made her more nervous than she had anticipated. *He can probably sense my nerves,* she thought, as the hug lingered. He removed his hands from around her waist and reached behind his neck to grab hers. She fell back on her heels as he took a step back, holding her hands in his. Melissa looked into his eyes for several beats, trying to calculate his next move. Just as she was about to blurt out "Good night!" and run inside, J.D. took her left hand in his and brought it up to his lips. He closed his eyes and gently kissed the top of her hand.

"Thank you for a lovely evening. I hope we can do this again," he said.

"Me, too," Melissa replied. Then J.D. winked as he released her hand and trotted down the front walk toward the road. Melissa wasn't sure what had just happened, but she knew one thing for sure: she was absolutely smitten.

THE FIFTH LETTER

March 3, 1977
Dear Mother,

So much has happened since we talked at Christmastime. I'm writing this letter from our new home—an apartment in downtown Los Angeles. Clark's cousin was evicted from the house where we were staying. Not to bore you with all the details, but we were nearly homeless. I have never been so frightened in my life. I truly thought we were going to be forced to live out of our car. Fortunately, one of Clark's foremen knew of a reasonably priced apartment, and we moved in immediately. He even helped us move, which was a huge relief because I'm not able to take my eyes off Ciarán for two seconds these days! Now that it is behind us, I can soundly say that it all worked out for the best. Clark's cousin, as amazing as he was for taking us in when we first moved here, had been acting very oddly of late. I had become skeptical of the model he was setting for our impressionable little boy, so I'm ultimately glad we were able to move out of there when we did.

Our new apartment is a bit smaller. Well, it's no Shangri-la by any means, but on the bright side, it is centrally located to so much that the city has to offer. For instance, I only have to take one bus instead of three to get to work now, which shortens my commute by almost an hour! And the market is within a much shorter walking distance, too. Silver linings everywhere!

103

As for Ciarán, he is getting so big. I understand the term "Terrible Twos" now, as we are in the thick of them. His temper tantrums are second to none, to the point where I don't take him out to run errands with me much anymore other than the library, which seems to soothe him from time to time. I've checked out so many books on how to parent a toddler, the librarians know me on a first-name basis now. I have read every tip and trick offered in the books, but so far nothing has worked. Consistent naps, rewards, time-outs, positive reinforcement . . . none seem to work very well. Clark is convinced that this is just a phase that he is going through, but he is seldom around during the day to see the full extent of Ciarán's behavior. I am trying to remain patient and understand that he is just a little boy, but some days he really tests me. He is lucky he is so adorable, and I tell him this all the time.

Now, I can only imagine what you must be thinking as you are reading this letter and envisioning the mess that your daughter has ended up in. I never said that I chose the easy path forward, but as a parent, I now see that this is what you were trying to protect me from. I'll be transparent and say that I don't know if I would have changed the course of my life if I knew then what I know now. I love my little boy immensely, but some days I can't help but wonder if I'm cut out to be a mother . . . his mother. If you have any advice on what to do, I'd take it in a heartbeat.

Love,
Ophelia

CHAPTER SIXTEEN

Friday, July 3

"Knock, knock!" Bethany called out as she opened Eleanor's front door. She had walked across this same threshold dozens of times before, but now she felt as if she were entering a strange and unknown place.

"I'm back here!" Julianne's voice called out from the study.

Out of habit and respect for her departed neighbor, Bethany began to slip off her tennis shoes, as she's always done in the past. As she was doing so, she froze momentarily, remembering the catastrophic state of the room where she was going, and put them back on. "Sorry. You understand," she whispered to Eleanor as she walked back to the study.

Although she knew the room was a disaster zone after the police inspection, the sight of it up close and personal made her stomach flip.

"Here you go. One frozen double-shot mocha with extra whip." She handed over a plastic to-go cup with Neptune's logo, a golden trident encased by a circle of coffee beans. Julianne took a long sip from the straw.

"Mmm. That is exactly what I needed. I'll pay you back later," she said. Bethany waved her hand dismissively as she sipped from her own straw.

"So, what's the plan of attack?" Bethany asked, looking around the room at the cleanup project at their feet. On the floor, torn pieces of paper were randomly strewn among fractured pieces of furniture, shards of broken glass, and stuffing that had once been inside Eleanor's leather couch before it was ripped to shreds.

"The officers told me to collect as much of the paper as possible in order to salvage any important documents that might still be here. We can pile those on the desk, and I'll go through them later. Once all the paper is picked up, I'm going to use Richard's industrial vac from the shop to clean everything else off the floor." Julianne paused before continuing. "Then, we'll take the furniture out to the garage to be hauled away later."

"That sounds like a plan, all right," Bethany said before taking another sip of coffee. "Where should I start?"

Julianne pointed across the room as she grabbed a broom to corral the loose papers that were scattered across the floor. Bethany moved carefully toward the fireplace. As she crouched down, she looked up at the wall above her and noticed that the ornately framed canvas portrait of Julianne had been slashed with a sharp object multiple times. She wondered if Julianne had noticed. She decided she would do whatever she could to distract Julianne.

"You'll never believe what happened to me at Neptune's this morning," Bethany started to say, as she moved away from the portrait. Julianne didn't respond other than to slightly cock her head sideways and raise her eyebrows as she focused on the task at hand.

Bethany continued. "The new barista? I'm pretty sure he hit on me."

"What?" Julianne's drawn-out one-word response sounded too incredulous. She quickly added, "I mean, not that I'm surprised that a guy would hit on you." *Good save,*

Julianne. "Give me the details!"

Bethany told the story. Neptune's was completely empty when she walked in, almost eerily so. When she ordered their drinks, she started chatting with the tatted-up guy working behind the counter. Bethany could tell immediately that he was from Southern California, so she felt a type of unexplained affinity toward him.

"He was laying the charm on real thick, I'm telling you. Right out of the gate," Bethany commented. As he was making their drinks, he was handing out compliments left and right. Although she was openly flattered, she assumed this was the tactic he had learned to squeeze tips out of people vacationing on the island. But as she pulled a crisp five-dollar bill to add to the tip jar, he put his hand over the lid and inched the jar away from her.

"Not necessary, darlin'. Seeing you again is all the payment I need. I hope you'll stop in again soon." He flashed a coy smile out of the corner of his mouth and winked at her.

Bethany thought about ending the flirtation right then and there by telling him she was in a committed relationship. But something stopped her. What's wrong with a little old-fashioned coquetry to spruce up one's self-esteem now and then? She smiled back and turned around to leave.

"As I left, I even think I heard him mutter to himself, 'Hate to see them go, but love to watch them leave.'" Bethany cinched her brows together and cringed.

"Ew! Creepy!" Julianne exclaimed as she continued cleaning.

"I know, right?" Bethany agreed.

"And you said this guy is new?" Julianne asked.

"I've seen him around Neptune's for the past—oh, I don't know—month or so? He hasn't been here long. I don't know what his story is other than he's as cocky as he is cute."

"Hmm," said Julianne. And they left it at that.

They were making a lot of progress and, after only an

hour, had most of the papers picked up and placed in neat stacks on the desk. Eleanor, Bethany realized, had kept almost every paper of consequence that she'd encountered in her lifetime: billing statements from doctor's offices and utility companies, health insurance plan documentation, and even the paperwork that accompanied her prescription medication. Eleanor had it all. What they didn't find, however, was any paperwork related to her will or estate.

"Maybe she kept it in a different room. Does she have a safe hidden somewhere in the house?" Bethany asked.

Julianne had explored every nook and cranny of the house when she played hide-and-seek with her dad as a young girl. If there was a safe or a secret area in the house, she would have discovered it ages ago.

"No, I don't think so. It would have been here," Julianne said defeatedly. She knew the likelihood of finding the will—or any related paperwork—was slim. As she reached for a dustpan, she realized that she was more upset by the fact that she had let herself maintain any hope that they would find something more than they did.

"We'll find it," Bethany said confidently.

Julianne wasn't so sure.

CHAPTER SEVENTEEN

An anomalous heat wave had washed over Jade Island, and without any windows to open inside the boarded-up study, Bethany and Julianne could only work in short spurts before needing to cool off and rehydrate. To get some fresh air, they retired to the shady porch next door for a midday snack. Julianne took a shower while Bethany made fresh lemonade and prepared a platter of cucumber and pimento cheese sandwiches.

They had worked up more of an appetite than they had thought. After they cleaned the platter between them, they decided to take a break before going back to work on the study. They were down to one garbage bag, so Julianne grabbed her wallet and the keys to Eleanor's car and headed to the square.

She parked Eleanor's car across from the Book Cellar. From the front seat, she peered through the windshield and watched Richard, sitting behind a computer screen at the checkout counter, lost in a book. She decided not to disturb him and took off in the opposite direction to the island's market instead.

Jade Island Market was full of people—locals and vacationers alike—grabbing last-minute provisions for their

Fourth of July cookouts and fireworks-watching parties. Julianne scanned the signs above each aisle until she saw the one she needed. Aisle 9: Cleaning Supplies. She weaved between shoppers and shopping carts before making a beeline to the only item she needed. As she stood in the aisle, studying the colorful boxes of trash bags, she felt the hair on her arms raise. Suddenly, she was less concerned about getting the best deal.

She was being watched.

She slowly looked left, then right, along the narrow aisle, and realized she was alone. *Stop it,* Julianne told herself. The overactive imagination that she'd had as a child would creep up on her as an adult from time to time. She slowly ran her hands down both of her arms and shook off the feeling. Distracted, she gave up on bargain shopping, picked the cheapest box of trash bags, and walked toward the register.

Julianne paid for her item and started walking out of the store. She reached for the phone in her back pocket, bumping her elbow into the person behind her.

"Sorry," Julianne politely said in motion, barely turning around.

"Julianne, right?" the person asked. It was Sam, the writer she had met at the bookshop the other day.

"Sorry, I didn't mean to elbow you back there. I should pay more attention to what I'm doing."

"No worries." Sam laughed it off. Gesturing toward the box of trash bags in Julianne's hand, they said, "Looks like you got out of there doing a lot less damage than most folks."

"Oh, yeah. Just doing some cleaning." Julianne paused, and a moment of awkwardness settled between them. Outside of a hospital setting, Julianne was never good at making small talk. And it seemed like Sam wasn't either. Trying to ease the growing discomfort between them, Julianne added, "I'm going to go over to see Richard before

I head home." *Lie.* "Want to join me?"

"That sounds great," Sam said.

The truth was, having seen Richard engrossed in his book, Julianne hadn't planned on stopping there. Sam hadn't either. They both had other plans to keep them plenty busy today, but the suggestion served as an easy way to break the awkward tension. *I'll just spend a few minutes at the Book Cellar before continuing the cleaning spree,* Julianne promised herself.

The island was flooded with people for the holiday weekend. As Julianne and Sam darted around tourists along the sidewalk, Julianne talked about this being her favorite time of year on the island.

"Even with all these people?" Sam asked.

"*Because* of all these people, in fact. As a kid, this place felt quite empty and boring between Labor and Memorial Days."

"Ah, so you live here year round?"

"I *did.* Not anymore," Julianne corrected them.

"Did you go to school here?" Sam inquired.

"I sure did. Jade Island Academy." Julianne extended her index finger toward the north. "There were eleven of us in my graduating class. We were one of the bigger grade levels, believe it or not."

"Wow. That is much different from the eleven *hundred* in my senior class," Sam commented. They couldn't imagine going to such a small school. There would be no way to blend in and fly under the radar like Sam had.

They arrived at the Book Cellar a moment later. Julianne relished the blast of air-conditioning that hit the front of her as she opened the door.

"Well, look what the cat dragged in. I am surprised to see the two of you," Richard replied.

"It feels wonderful in here, Richard," she said.

"I aim to please."

"We just happened to run into each other at the

market," Sam said.

"Literally!" Julianne blurted. *What an awkward thing to say. Geez, why can't you act normal?*

"Well, it's good to see you both. Sam, how is the, uh, writing coming along?" Richard stammered.

"Oh, pretty good, I guess you could say," they said, bobbing their head up and down.

Julianne couldn't put her finger on it, but there was something that felt off about Richard's and Sam's body language. *Why does this whole encounter feel so strange?* Julianne wondered.

"To be honest, the heat was distracting me, so I came down to the town for a break. People watching does wonders for the soul."

"Understood. We've been so busy, I haven't had a chance to step outside. It looks like a warm one, though," Richard replied. Julianne and Sam nodded exaggeratedly.

"Where are you staying, Sam?" Julianne asked.

"I'm renting an apartment down the street. I've been told it is known around here as the Flamingo House. Know it?"

"Of course! That's Ms. Townsend's house. She was my English teacher," Julianne said.

"Oh, cool! She's great and so welcoming. Everyone here has been wonderful so far," said Sam. In their young career, they had already worked in a handful of towns that weren't so inviting to newcomers. Sam assumed there was something about their lightly gelled and perfectly coiffed purple hair, nose ring, and dark eye makeup that unsettled some folks, especially older people. And if that didn't do it, Sam's uniquely epicene fashion—usually consisting of floral or paisley button-ups, cropped dungarees, and Doc Martens—would stir intrigue, which usually led to gossipy whispers that eventually became the soundtrack playing in the background of Sam's work.

So far, that wasn't the case on Jade Island. People here were different.

Richard had broken away from the conversation to ring up a customer. Julianne looked down at her watch. "I should probably get going. Bethany and I hope to have most of this cleanup job done by nightfall."

"Need any help?" Richard and Sam asked in unison. They looked at each other and smirked. Julianne wasn't in a place to turn down help, but most of what they had left to do was moving bulky, heavy furniture into the garage—not a task for a man in his eighties or an island visitor.

"I appreciate the offer—"

"Now, I want you to think *real* hard before you turn us down," Richard said, reading her mind. "How about I bring over a couple of pizzas after I close up? To feed the hungry?"

Julianne acquiesced graciously and walked out of the bookstore and into the oven-like temperatures. As she gently closed the door behind her, she saw Sam whisper something to Richard. She wasn't sure what they were up to, but she was curious to find out.

CHAPTER EIGHTEEN

Julianne knew every road on the island like the back of her hand. She knew where every manhole cover, curb, and crack in the asphalt was. But when it came to sitting in the driver's seat, traveling the one-and-a-half miles from the square back to Grammy's was like traversing a new path for the very first time.

Unlike most sixteen-year-olds, and despite her parents' best attempts to teach Julianne to drive that last summer, Julianne saw no point in getting her driver's license right away. She had never *needed* to drive anywhere on her own. Anyway, she *preferred* to travel on foot or on her bicycle most of the time. It wasn't until she was a junior in college and looking for off-campus apartments with Jenny that she finally admitted that a car would make her life much more convenient. Jenny was the one to teach her how to drive, and even went with her to take her driver's test. And two weeks later, Jenny sat next to her as she bought her first car, a white 1999 Ford Taurus with seventy-five thousand miles on it, which the girls affectionately named Betty (White). As Julianne signed her name on the paperwork, all she could think about was how much she wished she had just agreed to let her parents teach her how to drive all those years ago so she could have shared this moment with them.

Julianne pulled her new car into the carport, where it sat for weeks as she sunk into a small depression. A depression from which no one—not Grammy or Jenny or any of Julianne's other friends—could extract her. Perhaps it was the overwhelming process of learning to drive and buying a vehicle of her own, or just the mere thought that she did it all—as she did everything those days—without the guidance of her parents, that had consumed her happiness. Either way, it wasn't until her first week of classes that she managed to pull herself out of that funk by necessity, in order to make sure she could still apply for medical school, her parents' dream for their daughter.

Julianne was abruptly knocked out of her recollection when the car reached the top of the driveway. The garage door was partially lifted, with just enough space for a body to crawl underneath.

I know that door was closed when I left. The burglars . . . they must have returned. Should she go in and inspect, or would she be met with danger? Her brain was telling her to park the car and race next door. Her gut was telling her something else. *Face them,* Julianne told herself. Using the garage door remote attached to the visor above her head, she opened the door. As the large door slowly crawled up into the ceiling, Julianne noticed that the garage was filled with furniture . . . the furniture from Eleanor's study.

Before Julianne could make sense of what she was seeing on her own, Bethany walked up to the car with a floor lamp in her hand.

"Hey!" Noticing the concerned look on Julianne's face, she quickly said, "I hope you don't mind . . . I didn't want to lose steam from all the progress we made this morning, so Alex came over and helped me move some of the furniture out."

Julianne got out of the car. "No, that's great," she

said. "How did you get into the house?"

Bethany shrugged. "The front door was unlocked."

Julianne didn't remember leaving the house so vulnerable. Ever since the break-in, she had locked every door behind her, even briefly locking Alex out of his own house earlier that week. *I could have sworn I locked the door behind me.*

She followed Bethany through the house and into the study. Bethany had swept most of the remaining large debris into neat piles to be loaded into the bags once they arrived. And the portrait of her as a seventeen-year-old—which had been slashed to smithereens—was off the wall and out of sight. *Thank goodness.* She had never liked that portrait, but she never dared to fight Grammy over it.

"Richard is going to be here shortly with pizza," Julianne announced as she tossed the box of garbage bags toward Bethany. Bethany caught the box in one hand and gave a thumbs-up with the other. "Nice catch. You've made good progress without me."

"Alex did most of it. He didn't have any more calls this afternoon due to the holiday, so he came over and helped."

Just then, Alex walked into the room with his hands up in the air. "I heard my name . . . I swear I didn't do it!"

"Bethany was actually giving you credit for all the progress that's been made here this afternoon," said Julianne. As she spoke, she wondered where in the house Alex was when she'd arrived. He hadn't made a peep before entering the room.

"Oh. Well, in that case . . ." Alex reached for Bethany's waist and pulled her close before planting a long kiss on her cheek. Bethany put her hands on both sides of his stubbled cheeks and kissed him back on the lips. Bethany and Alex's relationship reminded Julianne of her parents. She hadn't known them very long, but from what she'd seen they were more than a couple—they were a team. Every decision they made, they made together. They rarely argued, and if they did it wasn't for long. Julianne would catch them stealing loving glances at each other when the other person wasn't looking. As far as she could tell, they were perfect together. It was a relationship Julianne had dreamed of having one day—that is, before her parents died. Since that fateful day, she'd accepted being on her own. It was better that way.

They continued working on moving furniture for a while longer until the front doorbell rang. At the same time, Julianne's phone began to ring with an unknown number. "I'll get the door, you take the call," Bethany said as she put down her broom and jogged toward the front of the house.

Bethany heard Julianne answer her phone in the study as she entered the foyer. Just then, the front door creaked open. "Hello!" Richard shouted out as he pushed the door ajar with his foot. His arms were full of stacked pizza boxes from Antonio's. Behind him was Melissa, who held a plate of freshly baked cupcakes, and Sam, who was balancing three two-liter soda bottles in their arms.

"Hi, guys!" Bethany welcomed them as she reached for the pizza boxes to lighten Richard's load. As they filed into the kitchen from the front of the house, Alex and Julianne joined them from the study in the back. Once they circled around the oversized island, Richard introduced Sam to everyone.

"I'm glad you could join us," Julianne said. "That was the window installers who just called. They'll be here on Monday to install the new windows."

"Wow, that's fast," Bethany said.

"The owner of the company knew Grammy pretty well. They are doing a rush order over the holiday."

"Your grandmother was one heck of a lady. Anyone would do *anything* for her," Richard said.

"Which makes what happened here a few days ago—

and the reason for the windows in the first place—such a mystery," Melissa said, as she exchanged looks with Julianne. Alex and Bethany looked at each other as well, as did Richard and Sam.

The party of six each grabbed a few slices of pizza, poured themselves something to drink, and took their overflowing paper plates and paper napkins into Eleanor's formal dining room. Julianne hadn't eaten between these four walls since she was in high school. It was Christmas Day, and her mother had begged Grammy to use her fine china to serve the large feast, which was fit for a king or queen. That was the last time a hearty home-cooked meal was ever made in that house. But now, something about eating pizza on a paper plate in this same room, disconnected her from her past dining experiences in this room.

"Does everyone have plans for tomorrow's holiday?" Richard asked once they were all settled in their seats.

"Well, tomorrow is our anniversary," Alex shared. Everyone around the table oohed and aahed. "Yes, yes, yes. Thirteen years. Can you believe it?" he added, before leaning into Bethany and playfully shooting her a smoldering look of desire. Bethany rolled her eyes before daintily pecking him on the lips and pushing him away.

"What are you doing to celebrate?" Melissa asked.

Bethany explained that for the past five years, Alex had chartered a romantic catamaran cruise to sail them around the island and watch Jade Island's fireworks display from the water.

"That sounds amazing," Melissa said dreamily.

Everyone took turns sharing their Fourth of July plans. Sam announced they were planning on staying at the apartment to get some work done, and Richard was gathering with some of his friends from the Jade Island Chamber of Commerce at North Beach Park. After Melissa excitedly shared that her in-laws were bringing her kids to the island for a cookout, everyone turned to look at Julianne.

"I guess I don't have plans for tomorrow. I'll probably go for a run and then watch the fireworks from the front porch." Being so high up on the bluffs, Julianne used to love sitting in the front yard, feeling like she was a keeper of the island. She would make up magical stories about what was happening on the streets below. "Watching those fireworks was one of my favorite family traditions," she added quietly before taking another bite of her pizza.

Everyone exchanged quick knowing glances at one another. Nobody wanted Julianne to feel alone on the holiday. Finally, Melissa spoke up.

"You know what, Jules? You do have plans. Fel and Margaret would love to see you again. And I would love for you to meet Carson and Lily. Come on over for the barbecue tomorrow. Please?"

Julianne looked around the table at five sets of hopeful eyes looking at her sympathetically. "I don't want to be an imposition—"

"Nonsense!" Melissa cried out. "It would be an honor to have you there. I think we are eating around three or four in the afternoon, but you can come over anytime. It'll be fun!"

A grin slowly emerged on Julianne's face. Something about seeing Fel and Margaret after all these years filled her heart with the warmth of nostalgia. Melissa took the absence of Julianne's retort as an acceptance of her invitation, so she left it at that.

As Melissa reached for her cup to take a victory swig of soda, she felt her phone vibrate in her back pocket. She reached behind her and peeked at the screen. J.D.'s name popped up. This was the first she had heard from J.D. since their date last night. Throughout the day, she felt increasingly nervous that maybe that awkward moment they'd shared on the front porch was enough to deter him from wanting to ask for a second date. She shoved her phone and the distraction back into her pocket.

"What was that?" Bethany asked from across the table.

"What was what?" Melissa replied.

"What just happened that made your face light up like a Christmas tree?" Bethany laughed.

Melissa decided denial was her best option for now. "I have no idea what you are talking about," she replied, her voice sounding monotone and robotic. *Wow, I'm a horrible liar.*

"Yeah, okay . . ." Bethany said slyly. She decided to drop the topic but not before giving Melissa a knowing wink. She'd pursue this later.

After they cleared their plates, Richard suggested that they finish cleaning up the study.
Everybody got to work, and by the time the sun was setting, the room was in good shape.

"Not bad for a day's work," Alex said as they walked out of the house. Bethany reached up and gave him a high-five. The cloudless sky looked as if it had been smeared with a Bomb Pop, the red warmth of the sun fading to white and then to blue. The lampposts on the street flickered on, indicating that dusk was finally upon them.

"I know I must sound like a broken record by now, but I can't thank you all enough for your help," said Julianne. Richard and Bethany sandwiched her in a hug. Before she knew it, all six of them were huddled together in a big squeeze ball. She hadn't expected it, but all her concerns melted away momentarily. For the first time in a very long time, Julianne didn't feel alone.

THE SIXTH LETTER

June 4, 1980
Dear Mother,

We just survived the last week of preschool, which was a feat for us if I'm being honest. Ciarán tends to get along with other children (mostly), but according to his teachers, he struggles to listen and follow directions. Part of me is relieved because before he started school, I thought it was me, that there was something wrong with me and my inability to parent my own child. The only reassurance I feel is when Ciarán disobeys Clark, too. Clark doesn't let Ciarán's temper tantrums rile him up like I do, but he also deals with it a lot less. He remains so even-keeled, even when Ciarán is having the worst day. Apparently the preschool teachers and I don't have the same tolerance as my loving husband.

While part of me feels relief that I'm not alone, the other part of me is frightened for what is to come when Ciarán starts kindergarten in the fall. I was called only a handful of times this year to pick him up from school, which is, I'm sure, a handful more than other children's parents. I'm lucky my job has allowed me to take time from work to attend to my son. But those phone calls from his teachers are so embarrassing. This is not a pattern I want to continue.

You've provided sound advice to me in the past, and I hope that there is more in your well of wisdom. We have a checkup with his

121

pediatrician at the end of the month, and I'll ask her for some advice, too. In the meantime, I ask that you join me in prayer that this is a phase that he'll grow out of very soon.

Love,
Ophelia

CHAPTER NINETEEN

Saturday, July 4
The thick slate-gray clouds held still over the island, keeping the first signs of sunrise a secret from all the early risers on the American holiday. Melissa was sound asleep, enjoying the most peaceful slumber of her adult life, when her cell phone began vibrating on the nightstand.
Buzz.
Buzz.
Buzz.
Buzz.

By the fourth loud staccato humming of her nightstand, she was awake. She figured Carson, who was usually up before the birds, was texting her from his grandmother's phone, a habit he had recently picked up while staying at her in-laws'. She rubbed the sleep out of the corners of her eyes. As her eyes adjusted to the blue light radiating from the screen, she discovered that it wasn't Carson messaging her. It was J.D.

She had fallen asleep the night before as they texted back and forth. It reminded her of the early days of her long-distance relationship with Chris, when she would routinely wake up to the cordless phone next to her ear and a static dial tone on the other end. She reached for her phone and opened her text messages.

5:37AM

Good morning darlin

I hope you slept well. I have to open Neptunes

Do you have any plans to watch the fireworks tonight?

If not maybe we can watch them together?

Most of their texts yesterday were flirtatious banter, but they hadn't laid any foundation for a second date. As Melissa propped herself up in the bed, the one that she'd shared with Chris for many years, she wasn't even sure that she wanted or deserved a second date. One romantic evening with a very handsome man and some cheeky texts seemed like more than enough to inflate her self-esteem back to healthy levels. A second date would be a nice bonus, but did she really need to see him a second time?

She looked at the selfie that he had sent above the string of texts. He was stretched out on a velvet green couch, shirtless. His hand was behind his head, revealing a toned bicep and his muscular chest. She zoomed in on the photo to look at his tattoos more closely. She noticed a wolf on his shoulder and a feather along his rib cage. The other tats, she assumed, were generic designs that she had seen variations of over the years in movies or in celebrity tabloids. *Boy, he is handsome,* Melissa thought to herself, *and he knows it.* The dozens of Lifetime movies she had watched taught her that that combination usually spells trouble. But again, she didn't foresee any long-term relationship with J.D. Or did she?

She really didn't want to turn down his offer to watch fireworks, but it was out of the question with Fel, Margaret, and the kids coming for the cookout. She didn't know for sure, but she couldn't imagine that they'd leave before Jade Island's firework show that evening.

Plus, she was on this island for another week. If she

turned him down, that would make for a very awkward reunion anytime she wanted to stop at Neptune's for coffee, which was almost daily she now realized.

She began typing her reply.

Good morning. 😊 *That sounds like a lovely evening, and I would enjoy it very much, but I have family visiting today. Can I take a rain check?*

She felt bad as soon as she sent it. *What if he doesn't take rejection well? What if my "rain check" comment seems too presumptuous?* She was putting a lot of stock into the reaction of a guy she dated once and may not ever date again. Just as she was contemplating writing something else, she saw the three dots pop up on her screen. A moment later, his response came through.

For you? Of course.

Let me know what works for you darlin

Whew. Apparently, J.D. was as understanding as he was handsome. *A second date is definitely happening,* Melissa thought as she rolled out of bed.

CHAPTER TWENTY

The Santanas' bronze SUV rolled up the driveway at ten thirty on the dot, just as Margaret predicted when they'd left the house. *How in the world does she do that?* Melissa asked, not that she should be surprised. Margaret was the ultimate planner. It was almost as if she directed the ferry according to her plans, too. As soon as the vehicle parked, Melissa ran down the wide front porch steps toward the stone-paved driveway. She pulled open the back-seat door to cheers from both her children. "Mommy!" they shouted excitedly.

"My babies!" Melissa shouted through joyful tears. She had prepared for the emotional reunion ever since she got off the phone with them the night before. It had only been a week since she left them at Fel and Margaret's, but it felt like months.

She covered Lily in kisses as she got her out of her booster seat and then wrapped Carson in her arms as soon as he climbed out of his side of the car. He normally struggled to break free of her mama-bear hugs, but this time she noticed that he hung on to her awhile longer. It both warmed and broke her heart a little. She was so thankful to see her little boy, who, she noticed, was looking more and more like Chris.

"How was the drive?" Melissa asked.

"It wasn't too bad—I was pleasantly surprised. It was a good thing we booked our ferry pass when we did," Fel said.

"The ferry was packed. I told you it would be," Margaret added. She gently squeezed Melissa's shoulders with her perfectly manicured hands, followed by a dainty kiss on each cheek, careful not to ruin her perfectly applied makeup. For as long as Melissa could remember, Margaret had always been the epitome of put together. Hair? Roots always touched up on the third Tuesday of the month. Nails? Manicured every other Wednesday. Clothes? Always dry-cleaned and pressed. Calendar? Kept up to date by the hour. Vacations? Always booked one year in advance with the travel agent. Before having kids, Melissa dreamed of following in Margaret's footsteps. Nowadays, she was lucky if she even remembered to swipe on some lipstick in the morning when she took the kids to school.

Fel grabbed the bags from the trunk of the car and ushered the rest of the family toward the front door of the house. "We've got a barbecue to prepare for!"

Melissa led her kids into the family room and unloaded their bags of toys onto the plush area rug. They rarely traveled to their grandparents' house—or any family members' homes—without their go-to forms of entertainment: Legos, Pokémon cards, Littlest Pet Shop sets, and some of Melissa's hand-me-down Barbies. Lily knelt down on the floor immediately and started building with the Legos. Carson joined her for a moment before running up to Melissa.

"Mom, can I have your phone?" he entreated. She had never given her kids digital devices before, having read up on the long-term effects of overexposure to screens. She knew that Margaret didn't read those articles and handed her phone over quite frequently to her grandkids. Cell phones were the modern-day babysitter, after all.

"No, honey. No cell phones today. Let's just hang out! Don't you want to build something with your Legos?" She tried to sound excited, but Carson hung his head in disappointment.

"Carson, this is a no-phone house. Grandma's rules," Margaret announced sternly, eager to assuage the situation. With that, the sad look on Carson's face lifted a bit, and he shrugged his shoulders before going back to help his sister with her build.

Melissa looked at her mother-in-law. "You know you created that monster, right?" She was careful with her tone, not wanting to sound too indignant or ungrateful.

"I know, I know. I told him that he can only use phones at Grandma and Grandpa's house," Margaret whispered back. Melissa was grateful that Carson and Lily had such caring grandparents who doted on them and enjoyed spending time with them. Growing up, Melissa didn't see her grandparents often, as they lived on the other side of the country. In hindsight, that was the driving force for Chris and Melissa to move back to Washington early in their relationship. She wanted her children to not only know their grandparents but grow up being loved by them. As she watched Margaret enthusiastically interacting with Carson and Lily as they brought their colorful bricks to her by the handful, Melissa knew they had done the right thing.

While Margaret played with the grandkids inside, Melissa moved to the back patio, where Fel was placing his famous barbecued ribs in the smoker. She reached into the cooler and grabbed two beers.

"It has been too long since I used this baby. I miss 'er," Fel said, as he tapped the lid of the smoker with the tongs. He reached for one of the beers in Melissa's hand.

"You know you could just get a smoker to have back at home," Melissa said.

"Yeah. I don't know about that, *mija*. The doctor told me I need to cut back in the meat department, and the lieutenant in there is always watching." He nodded toward the house. "She's made me eat more salads in the past year than I have in the last sixty years!" Fel playfully rolled his eyes.

"Well, that's a good thing. I wish I had someone around telling me to eat healthier. Unfortunately, my roommates are perfectly fine with frozen fish fingers, chicken nuggets, and tater tots for every meal." Her father-in-law chuckled before raising the bottle up to his lips.

"Hey, I invited Julianne over for your famous ribs. She didn't have a lot going on today, so I thought she might like to have some company."

"That's wonderful! There will be plenty of food, don't worry about that," Fel said.

"I was telling Margaret the other day that ever since Julianne got back to handle Eleanor's affairs, some really strange things have happened. Maybe you could give her some, you know, legal advice?"

"Margaret told me something about that. A missing will? And someone broke into the house? Which reminds me"—Fel looked up toward the roof—"I need to double-check the security system while we're here. I think the porch camera needs to be reset online again."

Oh no. Melissa's stomach dropped. She had forgotten about the security cameras around the house. Had her in-laws seen her and J.D.? Was Fel mentioning the front porch camera as a clue to his insider knowledge of what his daughter-in-law had been up to during her stay at his summer home? *Relax,* Melissa said to herself, as she took a deep breath. Knowing Margaret, if J.D. was seen on those cameras, she would have said something well before now.

To ease her mind and steady her heart rate, Melissa quickly changed the subject. She caught her father-in-law up on the details surrounding the break-in and the missing will, minimal as they were to her knowledge. As she was telling him the story about their trip to Port Forrester, she felt grateful to be part of a family full of lawyers; between her parents and her father-in-law, she never had to worry about legal matters. She knew it gave her a false sense of security as she went about her life in the real world, but it was security nonetheless, which was a valuable commodity these days.

CHAPTER TWENTY-ONE

"Felipe, my love, you've outdone yourself," Margaret said as she placed the last rib bone on her plate. Julianne and Melissa nodded in agreement. Fel's smoked ribs were second to none according to Melissa, and they had only improved year after year since that first summer her family vacationed at this house.

Fel wiped his face with a cloth napkin and threw it down next to his place mat. He leaned back in his patio chair and rested the back of his head on his intertwined fingers. "So, Julianne, Melissa tells me you've had quite a week. Tell me, where do things stand with your grandmother's affairs?"

Julianne had just spooned a mouthful of Margaret's famous pistachio pudding salad into her mouth, which gave her a moment to figure out how best to respond.

"That's a good question, to which I don't really know the answer. We went through her documents yesterday as we cleaned the study. Nothing of interest appeared, unfortunately. We suspect that the most important documents—her will, the deed to the estate, or even to the whole island—are long gone."

"Do the local police have any leads?" Margaret asked.

"If they do, they haven't shared any of them."

"Yeah, they haven't been the most useful so far," Melissa chimed in. Fel pursed his lips and bobbed his head, as though he wasn't surprised.

"Honey, what about Holice . . . Oh, what's his name?" Margaret tapped her fingers to her forehead trying to trigger her memory.

"Holice Bardell?"

"That's the one!" she exclaimed.

"He used to work for the state sheriff's department a while back. I can reach out to him Monday. See if he has any recommendations."

"What can he do that the local detectives can't?" Melissa asked.

"I'm not sure. But I suspect this case is out of the league of the fine folks who police this island. Jade Island has never seen a crime like this before." Julianne wondered if Fel had a point. Maybe they needed somebody else on the case.

"Julianne, dear, have you made memorial arrangements for your grandmother yet? Felipe and I would like to be here for that," Margaret said. When it came to grief or loss, her voice was always so delicate and gentle. Melissa remembered that most from when they'd lost Chris. It was like Margaret's words always floated softly through the air.

"Her wishes were to be cremated and to have her ashes spread under that big tree in the yard. We will have a service for her down at the chapel, and I believe Richard is discussing arrangements for a luncheon with some of the members of the chamber today. I'll make sure Melissa notifies you as soon as we have a date."

Margaret dropped her shoulder and tilted her head to the side. "Well, hang in there. I know that this is not an easy time for you."

Suddenly, Carson burst through the open patio doors to Melissa's side.

"Mom, who is Judd?" he asked. He had her cell

phone in his hand.

"Who, honey?" she asked, as she took her phone from him. As the words came out of her mouth, she knew the answer. She looked at her phone and realized that Carson had opened her text messages and saw J.D.'s name. He must have seen her texts. She gulped, wondering how much he understood. She immediately felt her cheeks flush with embarrassment.

"I took your phone, but it was *only* to text Grandma," Carson said, trying to reason with her, "and then Judd texted you a bunch of times. But I can't read it." Carson hung his head.

Instead of answering his question, Melissa scolded her son. "Carson, what did I tell you earlier about using my phone?"

He lifted his head halfway to respond to his mother. "No phones," he said ashamedly.

"Right," Melissa said. She knew she didn't have much more time with him this visit, and she didn't want her own embarrassment to make a bigger deal out of this than it was. She adjusted her tone to sound more forgiving. "So please listen next time. Okay?" She gave him a squeeze and kissed the top of his head.

Wanting to break up the tension, Julianne offered to go inside with Carson to play Legos with him and his sister.

"Really?" Carson asked, surprised.

"Are you kidding me? I love Legos!" Julianne replied. Carson took her by the hand and led her inside.

Margaret leaned toward Melissa. "You go inside with them. Enjoy some time with your babies. Felipe and I will clean up."

"Really?" Melissa echoed her son's surprise.

"Go," Fel instructed, as he shooed her from the table with his hands. As Melissa jogged inside, Fel poured Margaret another glass of chilled chardonnay. With their grandchildren playing inside, he reached for her hand, and they both took a sip of their chilled beverages. Before cleaning up, they decided to relish this quiet, relaxing moment under the canvas canopy of their lovely summer home.

Julianne and Melissa each refilled their own wine glasses as they walked through the kitchen into the family room, where colorful Legos covered the floor. In the middle of the room, Carson and Lily sat across from each other, working on different builds. Julianne sat cross-legged next to Lily and began to lock bricks together. Melissa kneeled next to Carson and helped him construct a building. "It's going to be a firehouse," Carson said imaginatively.

"I'm so lucky these two love playing together," Melissa said, as she fastened two bricks together.

"Did you play with your brothers growing up?" asked Julianne.

"Yes and no, but nowhere near as much as these two do. There was a bigger age gap between us, and the boys always had each other."

"Are you close now as adults?"

"No, not really. We all have our own families, and we're spread apart. My oldest brother, Mark, lives in Denver with his wife and kids. My other brother, Malcolm, and his husband, Taj, live in Portland. I'm the only one who stayed close to Mom and Dad."

"Ah."

"When we lost Chris, Malcolm and Taj would drive up every weekend to take care of me and the kids. They did that for a couple of months, actually. But then it was time for us to make it on our own, and they stopped driving up as frequently. Now, I think it has been eight or nine months since we've seen them. Everyone gets so busy," Melissa said, as she continued to add bricks onto Carson's firehouse.

Julianne had never told anyone that she'd always wanted a sibling. She didn't have many friends on the island growing up. She got along with her classmates, but there was always an unspoken chasm between her and them. She assumed it was her family's status on the island that made her seem untouchable or unreachable. Growing up, she considered her parents to be her best friends. If she had a sibling, she knew they would be her best friend. Her confidant. Her protector. The person who would have shared in her grief when her parents died and even now.

"It is wonderful that your kids are so close," Julianne said. "It is like having a built-in best friend. Isn't it?"

"For their sake, I hope so." Melissa sighed.

Melissa's phone vibrated on the floor beside her. The screen lit up again with a new text message from J.D.

Julianne couldn't help but look. "J.D., huh?"

Melissa noticed that both her kids were enthralled with their projects. She picked up her phone and read the message.

Just left work. Thinking of you darlin.

She couldn't help the smile that spread across her face from cheek to cheek. She put her phone in her back pocket. She would reply to him later.

Julianne repeated herself with more emphasis, "J.D., *huh?*"

"Yeah, just a friend I met here this week." She tried to sound as indifferent as possible, but Julianne saw right through it.

"Mel? C'mon, you ought to know me better than to think I'd buy that 'friend' nonsense," Julianne said.

"Well, nonsense or not, it is true. We met at Neptune's earlier in the week." Melissa was determined not to share too much, especially in front of her kids, but she couldn't help divulging a bit more. "And we may or may not have hung out after we returned from Port Forrester the other day."

Julianne's eyes widened. "Really, now? Well, that is an interesting development!"

"Yes. This *friend* is very nice." Melissa lowered her voice. "And very cute, I might add." Her smile grew bigger as she recalled how devilishly handsome J.D. looked on their first date the other night.

"And you said you met this friend at Neptune's? So I take it that they are a coffee drinker. Always a good sign!" Julianne joked.

"Yeah, well, my friend works there," Melissa added. It took Julianne a few seconds to register what she'd heard. Once she made the mental connection to her conversation with Bethany from the morning before, her facial expression suddenly turned from jovial to serious.

"He works there?" Julianne asked, seeking clarification.

"Yeah, he is working as a barista there this summer while he vacations on the island. He's taking some time away from California, where he's from."

Julianne sat back, and her mind began to race. *Don't jump to conclusions. I must be misunderstanding something,* she thought. *But what are the odds? Could this be the same guy who hit on Bethany yesterday? And if so, how do I find out?*

CHAPTER TWENTY-TWO

After Fel and Margaret cleaned up from the barbecue and Carson and Lily presented their completed Lego builds to everyone (a firehouse and a dog-grooming salon, respectively), Melissa's in-laws packed up the SUV and said their goodbyes. As it turned out, Fel wanted to get on the ferry before the fireworks display so that they wouldn't have to fight the crowds leaving the island later in the evening.

It was a tearful goodbye, as Melissa knew it would be. *One more week,* she kept mantra-ing to herself. While she hadn't been convinced at first, she was so grateful to have these two weeks to herself on the island. And she was even more grateful for her in-laws' generosity of lending her the house and driving all the way to Jade Island for a day trip with the kids. They would be dropping their grandkids off at Melissa's parents' house the following morning so they could reclaim their sanity. Carson and Lily were the sweetest children. Everyone Melissa knew said so. But still, their energy was . . . a lot. She knew that better than anyone.

Julianne left soon afterward, so she could get a twilight run in before the fireworks. Melissa had noticed something shift in Julianne's demeanor as they were playing with the kids that afternoon. She wondered if it was just weariness from the week's events or if it was something more. She would make a point to ask Julianne about it tomorrow.

Once the house was empty, Melissa reached for her phone. She decided to text "her friend" back and suggest they meet up to watch the fireworks after all. He responded right away.

Absolutely. Meet at your place?

Fel's comments about the security cameras replayed in Melissa's head. The house was off-limits now.

I want to get out of the house after spending all day here. Let's meet in the square instead.

J.D. didn't respond immediately to her idea to meet in a more public setting. As she waited for his reply, her mind speculated on what he might be thinking. A few minutes later, he replied.

OK. Meet me at Neptune's at 9.

Nine o'clock? That seemed pretty late to begin their date. It was past the time that Melissa usually began her bedtime routine. But this *was* a date to watch the fireworks. The first boom of detonation would go off around nine thirty. She supposed it wasn't unreasonable, so she sent three words back.

See you there.

CHAPTER TWENTY-THREE

Richard grabbed an ice-cold bottle of Coca-Cola from the cooler on the picnic bench and held it in his outstretched arm. "David?"

The friendly restaurateur took the ice-cold bottle from his friend, and then Richard took another for himself. Three of the sixteen members of the Jade Island Chamber of Commerce had walked down to the North Beach Park earlier in the day to reserve the picnic table for the cookout. By five in the afternoon, the chamber members and their families had gathered at the park with enough food to feed an army, as had been tradition for the past twenty years.

"So, Rich, how's Eleanor's granddaughter getting along? This must have been a really tough week. I couldn't believe it when I heard about the break-in—and to think it happened when you were at my place!"

"David, I have to say, it has been tense. But I'm tellin' you . . ." Richard paused deliberately, looked downward, and slowly shook his head. "That girl? She is a rock." He cast his eyes upward to look at David.

"Just like Eleanor," David said.

"Just like her," Richard confirmed.

David studied his friend with sincere eyes. "You miss

her."

"Well, we all miss her," Richard said.

"We do. The town has felt . . . duller. Our last chamber meeting lacked luster without her presence, no question about it." David put a hand on Richard's shoulder. "But you must feel that in spades compared to the rest of us. The two of you were like nothing I'd ever seen. True confidants. True companions. Like peanut butter and jelly. How the two of you only remained friends all these years is the world's greatest mystery."

"Not that again, Dave," Richard said exhaustedly. Shortly after moving to Jade Island and opening his bookshop, Richard had wanted to ask Eleanor out on a romantic date. And he almost did . . . once.

It was springtime. Richard was setting up a book display in the front window of his shop. Out of the corner of his eye, he caught a bright beam of sunlight reflecting off Eleanor's mahogany hair, which was neatly pulled back. He watched her every move as she moved through the park under a canopy of exploding cherry blossoms toward the Book Cellar. It wasn't until she paused for traffic across the road from his shop that he realized she was coming to see him. He quickly arranged the last stack of books. As she pushed open the door, Richard nervously tugged down on his shirt and ran a hand through his thick, wavy locks to smooth them back. Eleanor was unsuspecting of his efforts to look his best.

"Hello, Richard." Eleanor looked around, cataloging every detail of the space. "I wanted to stop by and see how you were getting along. The place looks lovely." Her tone was always professional, but Richard had noticed that it had grown warmer over their last few encounters.

"It's good to see you, Eleanor." Richard's breathing had noticeably intensified. *Good lord. Calm down, man.*

"And you as well, Richard." She peered into his eyes.

"Is something the matter?" It was like she could read his mind.

"No, not at all." With that, he saw her shoulders relax. "Well, actually, I wanted to ask you something."

Eleanor raised her eyebrows, seemingly intrigued. "Well, how providential. I also wanted to ask *you* a question."

"Ladies first," Richard said with a slight bow, gesturing his hand toward her.

"My daughter is looking for a part-time job."

Daughter? Richard thought to himself. *Eleanor has a daughter?* Richard had assumed, based on all his conversations with people in the community—including Eleanor—that she lived alone. He obviously didn't know as much about her as he thought he did.

"Anyway, she loves to read and is quite the writer. And I thought that you could use some help getting things 'up-and-running,' as they say. She could help with merchandising, advertising, stocking books, or whatever you need." Eleanor paused and waited for a reaction. Richard, scrambling to figure out what to say next, didn't say anything at all.

"Of course, this is just a proposal. You don't need to answer me now. But it would be a huge favor to me if you—"

"Yes, of course," Richard blurted out. "I definitely could use the help. That sounds like a great idea."

Eleanor looked pleased. "Thank you. There's one more thing . . ."

"Yes?"

"She is pregnant. My grandchild will be born later this year. I just wanted to be transparent with you, since this would be a favor to me and all."

Through Eleanor's stoic exterior, Richard could sense her excitement. His face softened. "Congratulations, Eleanor. Your family must be thrilled."

"Thank you, Richard. Yes, we are very excited for this next chapter." She grinned briefly before her face resumed its usual, serious expression. "I have to get going. But first, what did you want to ask me?"

"Oh, it was nothing important. It can wait." And it was a question that waited to be asked for almost thirty years and for the remainder of their friendship. For the first few years, Richard debated whether to propose a more romantic relationship to Eleanor. But after a few years, he lost the need. They had become such intimate confidants in almost every sense of the word, and Richard was going to do whatever he needed to do to protect that relationship, even if it meant keeping his romantic feelings hidden. He loved Eleanor and was certain she loved him in return. And that was all he wanted and needed in his life.

David wrapped Richard in a big, burly embrace, pulling Richard back to the present. "Tell ya what. I haven't been out on the water in weeks. How about we go out on the boat next week?"

"Sounds great, my friend," Richard replied softly. David walked over to the picnic table to fix himself a plate of food. Richard stood alone, watching the sun slide closer to the horizon. His mind went back to Eleanor and then to Julianne. He took a sip of his Coke and then, under his breath, he made a promise to his best friend: "I'm going to fix everything. I'm going to protect her, Eleanor."

CHATPER TWENTY-FOUR

The Matriarch's estate sat on the southern part of the Loop, a wide, smoothly paved eight-mile road that wrapped around the entire island. It gently rose up into the evergreen bluffs on the southern tip of the island before rolling down to the beach in the north. It was the perfect ribbon of asphalt for any moderate-to-serious bikers and joggers, and it was Julianne's most favorite road in the world.

"You have a favorite *road*," Jenny asked her once.

"Yes, doesn't everyone?" Julianne asked back.

"Well, I don't." Jenny thought for a moment. "But maybe I should."

When Julianne was a child, she would spend most summer evenings biking the Loop with her parents, as many families did. It was along the stretch that meandered through the towering Douglas firs that she discovered her love of running. Before joining the cross-country team her sophomore year of high school, she had spent most of her leisure time indoors with her books and CDs. Her petite size did not lend her to most contact sports, and the Great T-Ball Tragedy of '95 revealed she didn't have the best hand-eye coordination.

"What about cross-country?" her mom asked at

breakfast one summer morning as she flipped through the pages of Julianne's freshman-year yearbook.

"What about it?" Julianne asked.

"You enjoy going for walks with Daddy and me. Isn't running just a speedier walk?" Julianne kept her gaze on her to see if she was being serious. It appeared that she was.

"Maybe. But I don't know . . ." Julianne sounded despondent. Running seemed boring.

"Let's try it out, kiddo," her dad said as he approached the table with a plate of toast. "I'll run with ya."

The next day, they started training. Her dad helped her calculate a down-and-back distance from the house that was one mile in length for the first week, followed by three miles a few weeks later. By the end of the summer, they had calculated a challenging-yet-doable five-miler on the Loop. And when the school year began, Julianne had one of the best times on the team, and she shocked everyone when she beat the school's cross-country record her first season. Running became her passion and the one thing she could rely on to push her through some of life's toughest moments. Every time she went for a run, she imagined her dad running alongside her.

Running the Loop was a popular pastime for many other Jade Island residents, too. But on the evening of July Fourth, the Loop was eerily desolate as Jade Island settled in to watch its famous fireworks display. The lonely road called to Julianne, and she couldn't wait to have it all to herself.

She tied her shoes in double knots, threw her hair up in a high pony, and inserted her charged-up earbuds as she sauntered down the steep driveway. Julianne reached the road as the calypso beats from the first song on her eighties hits playlist—Lionel Richie's "All Night Long"—began to play. She looked to the left, then the right, and decided to take off to the west. It was the steepest section of road, which meant she would finish on a gentler incline coming back to the house.

Running was Julianne's escape from reality, back to a particular place that didn't exist. It gave her the sacred time and space to reconnect with her parents—the only people other than Jenny that she wholeheartedly trusted. She would imagine her mom at home, writing in her journal, playing her guitar, or enjoying afternoon tea with Grammy while trying to teach her how to knit for the thousandth time. Her dad was either running alongside her or back at home, taking notes while reading his latest *Kiplinger* or *Stocks & Commodities* magazines to the soundtrack of her mother's melodic strumming of the guitar. Alone on the road, Julianne would role-play various discussions with them out loud as she ran, like telling them about her day or asking them for career advice. As she talked with them, she was always playing her sixteen-year-old self, never a year older. And in every scenario, they had never gone on a road trip to California. In fact, when she was a teenager, she imagined that the California coast where they died had been hit by a meteor, wiping it off the map entirely, as if that would change her reality. After a few years, she grew out of needing to include that part of the story in her imaginative role-playing.

As she set up the scene for this particular run, she realized that this would be the first time she would be talking with her parents since she arrived on the island. She hadn't even sought their advice after the break-in—very uncharacteristic of her. She had so much to fill them in on, and she didn't even know where to begin.

Maybe you don't need to begin, her father said to her. He was running beside her.

"What are you saying?" Julianne said out loud to him.

Maybe you should let your friends help you with this one. You don't need us.

"I don't understand." Julianne stopped in the middle of the road, staring off into the distance.

You've turned to your mother and me for so many things. And that's mostly because you didn't have others to turn to. Now that you are back home—

"I'm not *back home*," Julianne said. "I'm here for now. Trying to figure everything out. Alone."

But you aren't alone. Open your eyes, Jules. Look at all the people around you that are there to support you.

Julianne threw her hands up in defeat. "Well, fine. But I don't need them. I *need* you and Mom."

She saw her dad grimace. She didn't need him to say what he was thinking. She knew what he would say, and she would rather not hear those words.

Let's just keep running, sweetheart. It's getting dark. She watched him look up at the streetlamps before waving his arm, encouraging her to keep moving.

She put one foot in front of the other and resumed her jog . . . alone. Through tear-filled eyes, Julianne could feel the stars shining down on her between the towering fir trees. Her favorite trees. She knew the fireworks would start soon, and she picked up her pace so she could make it back to the house before then. She could see the bend up ahead where the road started to gently rise above her. Years of cross-country training told her exactly where she was; she only had about three-quarters of a mile left to go.

Suddenly, a weird sensation came over her—the same feeling she'd had at the market the day before. She was being watched. Followed.

"Dad?" she let out, hoping it was him. She looked over her right shoulder, but the road was empty. She jogged a few more paces and then turned her head again. As her feet swiftly grazed the pavement that lay before her, she surveyed the dense area of trees that lined the street. Again, nobody was there.

Before she could turn her head back, it happened. Quicker than a lightning bolt.

Julianne's legs flailed backward first on impact. As her feet lifted from the ground, a darkened headlight crashed into her abdomen, propelling her body upward before gravity pulled it to the ground, landing on its side. A soft bed of fallen pine needles on the side of the road did their best to break her fall.

Julianne lay there, motionless and alone. After the set of screeching tires faded away, not a sound could be heard except for the electrical buzz of the streetlamps and the music that continued to stream through her earbuds.

CHAPTER TWENTY-FIVE

Melissa knew that parking anywhere near the square on the holiday would be an impossible task, so she decided to walk to Neptune's instead. While taking the car was easier, she loved the walk that meandered past all the Victorian homes and bungalows that gave the island its rich, historical feel. Melissa walked up the bluff past Bethany's house and turned right on Prospect Avenue, then followed the downward bend in the road toward Jade Island Avenue, made a quick left on Apple Lane, and followed that all the way to Main Street. She had taken this exact walk with her brothers when they were kids, and then hand in hand with Chris many years later, adding up to more times than she could count. As she got closer to the square, she noticed stars twinkling faintly in the eastern sky. The fireworks would begin shortly.

"Look at that excellent timing," J.D. said. He was walking from the opposite direction up the sidewalk toward Melissa. He leaned in and gave her an unexpected kiss on the cheek. She could feel his heart racing through his signature black V-neck. As he lingered close to her, she felt her heart pick up its pace, too. He held a brown paper grocery bag in one hand and grabbed her hand with the other. "Let's go," he said. He led them around the side of the coffee shop and opened a side gate entrance to the backyard. It was dark, but Melissa could see a staircase that led to the second floor above the coffee shop.

"Where are we going?" Melissa was as clueless about what J.D. had planned as she was about where the stairs were taking them.

"It's a secret," J.D. whispered. As he began to unlock the door at the top of the stairs, Melissa hesitated. The mommy in her that told her children to never be trusting of strangers wasn't sure she wanted to blindly follow him to whatever was on the other side of that darkened doorway. He opened the door, which revealed another door—likely to the apartment he was renting this summer—and a second set of stairs. "Almost there!" he said, as he started climbing. She swallowed her fear and faithfully followed.

When they got to the top, J.D. opened the hatch and revealed a wooden deck patio built on the top of the house. Melissa stepped out onto the patio and looked around, amazed.

"Wow! You can see everything from up here!" She could see specks of light sprinkled across the sound as hundreds of anchored boats waited for the fireworks to begin.

"It's not a bad little hideout," J.D. said. "And I can't imagine a more perfect place to watch fireworks." He placed the bag he had been holding next to the two folding deck chairs that he had set up for them.

Melissa continued to take in the panoramic views of the town below them before settling herself in one of the chairs. She hadn't even noticed that J.D. had opened a bottle of pink rosé and poured two glasses for them. He handed her a glass as he sat down.

"To you," he toasted. He sounded a bit out of

breath. But then again, they had just climbed two flights of stairs.

"Hmm . . . I feel like I've heard that before," Melissa said as she winked.

"And I mean every word of it." He winked back.

They took long sips of the rosé, savoring the refreshingly cool and citrusy beverage on the warm night.

"Delicious," Melissa commented. It was her third (okay, fourth, if she was being completely honest) glass of wine that she had enjoyed so far that day. It had been a very long time since she'd drank so much in one day. Even though she had been in the "feeling good" zone so far, she was unsure how she might react to this fourth (well, maybe fifth?) glass. Wanting to keep her wits about her, she placed the glass down on the deck so as not to be tempted to drink more.

J.D. didn't notice. He was consumed with swirling the wine in his glass like a professional sommelier. He pretended to study the wine in the light provided by the patio lighting strung above their heads. He seemed to be enjoying the show he was putting on for his date.

"How was time with the family today?" he asked.

"Oh, it was exactly what I needed to get me through the second half of this vacation," Melissa replied.

"Wasn't the whole purpose of your vacation to get away from your family?"

Melissa paused before asking, "Do you have kids, J.D.?"

"Nah," he answered quietly. "My buddies got a couple between them. I love 'em, but I never had any of my own."

"They flip your world upside down. As much as I enjoy my alone time, I crave time with them more. Especially now that they are young. I know that one day I am going to blink and their childhood will be over." She stopped, noticing that all the wine was making her overly sentimental. She hoped that J.D. would change the subject.

"I can't say I ever loved anything or anyone that much. But I'd like to try . . ." He reached over and pushed a fallen strand of her hair behind her ear. He lightly tugged on her chin with his thumb and forefinger, bringing her lips closer to his. As they grew closer and a kiss became more imminent, an explosion erupted in the sky above them, startling Melissa out of the moment.

"Oh, look! The fireworks have started!" Melissa jumped out of her chair and leaned on the patio railing. She had contemplated "the kiss" ever since meeting J.D. A part of her really wanted J.D. to kiss her, but something inside her was thankful for the distraction. He got up and stood next to her, following her gaze upward.

Above them, brilliant colors filled the night sky. Pink and white rays darted straight up, while gigantic neon-colored bombs exploded high in the sky before slowly cascading down toward the earth below. Melissa's favorites were the bright blue shooting stars that melted away into sizzling silver sparklers dancing above them. Standing there, she thought back to the last time she saw those fireworks. It was a few years ago when she watched them go off here on the island. It was the week that she and her husband found out she was pregnant with Carson but hadn't told anybody yet. It was standing under those fireworks when she felt she was falling in love with Chris all over again, this time as a dad.

Her memories had carried her away, as they did so often on this island. She tried to shake off the nostalgia and stay present in the moment. J.D. had tried to make their dates special and unique, and she wasn't ungrateful for that. But overcoming the wave of nostalgia on this day, especially after seeing her kids, was proving too difficult.

J.D.'s mysteriousness paired with his ridiculously

handsome features had lured her in. His charm almost got her to stay. But he had nothing when it came to the treasure trove of memories she had made with her family on this island. Jade Island belonged to her and Chris, at least for now.

Melissa turned to J.D. and looked deep into his eyes. She knew what she had to do.

"I have to go," she said. Without hesitating, she moved toward the hatch door. If she didn't put physical distance between them immediately, she wasn't sure she would be able to leave.

"What? Why?" J.D. asked with surprise.

"You've been lovely, J.D., but I'm just not ready to date yet."

"You are realizing that *just now*?" Melissa could sense the rejection irritated him. She thought about apologizing and trying to explain the feelings that had led her here. But what good would that do? It might heal his bruised ego enough that their next encounter at Neptune's would be less awkward. But it could open the door for him to convince her to stay.

"I think I've probably known it all along," she said, then turned around and left without another word.

THE SEVENTH LETTER

April 5, 1981
Dear Mother,

I'll start off with some good news. Really, it's the best news I've had in a while. You know that temporary position I took as a hostess at the steakhouse down the street? I've been promoted as the restaurant's new front-of-the house manager. Can you believe it? Now, it may seem like a small piece of news, but you know as well as I do that I don't have much of a managerial background. Despite that, the owner said he saw potential in me and wanted to give me a shot. Not only does this mean I get a raise in pay, but it also means I'll have more control over my schedule, which will allow me to take Ciarán to his therapy appointments, which are every other week.

His appointments have been going well, but he is struggling to fit in at school. We met with his teacher last week, who is recommending to the principal that Ciarán repeat kindergarten next year. She said that he is not socially mature enough to move on to first grade and is also behind in reading and writing. I was devastated at first and asked myself, How can this be my child? He is so smart and can be very charming, but he is also stubborn as a mule. And I don't wish any of his temper tantrums on my worst enemy. We've done everything I can think of to raise him to be a normal, healthy little boy. Yet I get the feeling that something is wrong.

I must admit that otherwise, we're doing well and are probably the most financially stable we've been since we moved to L.A. Of course, I attribute that to my husband's incredible work ethic. He continues to work tirelessly to provide for Ciarán and me. I'm hoping that we can continue to save up so that we can move into a new home sometime next year and maybe even consider expanding our family.

I miss you terribly and hope that you'll come down to visit us sometime. I know you are busy, so even if we don't get to see you, I'm grateful for every letter you send and all the advice that you share.

Love,
Ophelia

CHAPTER TWENTY-SIX

Sunday, July 5
"Breathe in . . . two . . . three . . . four. Breathe out . . . two . . . three . . . four," Bethany quietly chanted to herself.

She avoided hospitals at all costs. She'd discovered this irrational fear of hers on her seventeenth birthday. She had spent the afternoon surfing with a bunch of friends. They were standing along the shoreline with their boards when a sneaker wave hit. Bethany lost her balance and fell on a piece of driftwood behind her, shattering her arm in several places.

As the ambulance carried her off the beach, she began to hyperventilate. Watching *Grey's Anatomy* was the closest she had been to a hospital since the day she was born, and suddenly the thought of going to a hospital herself sent her into a panic. As they neared Scripps Hospital, the medics gave her a sedative just so they could roll her gurney into the emergency room when they got there.

From that day forward, Bethany did whatever she could to avoid hospital visits.

Richard had received the call just a few hours earlier. The fireworks had ended and everyone had retreated back to their homes or rentals. Richard shuffled into his apartment around one o'clock in the morning, moments after cleaning up after a lively outing with his friends on the commerce board. To settle in, he made some decaf Earl Grey tea and put a record on the turntable. Just as Duke Ellington's band began to play, Richard's phone rang. Officer Gupta was on the other end of the line, telling him that Julianne was currently being airlifted to the hospital.

Bethany took several sips of the rum and Diet Coke that she mixed before leaving the house as Richard drove them to the hospital in Port Townsend. The sun hadn't risen yet, and she still wasn't fully awake, but she wasn't taking any chances. "Nothing like a little liquid courage to help us overcome our demons," she told Richard on the drive. Richard nodded absentmindedly.

When they arrived at the hospital, they walked directly to the ICU, the same wing of the hospital where Richard visited Eleanor a week earlier. Richard noticed two uniformed police officers softly chatting in the hallway next to the nurses' station. Bethany and Richard approached Julianne's room. As he gently pushed on the door, a voice from behind them softly called out, "She's sleeping right now." They turned around and saw Detective Roberts standing behind them.

"Detective," Richard acknowledged. He tried to compose himself before saying, "Do you have any clue what is going on?" Bethany noticed Richard's face turning flush with concern.

"We're trying to figure that out right now." The detective spoke softly, attempting to invoke a sense of calm.

"With all due respect, there is someone targeting this family, and while you were doing god-knows-what to solve the break-in at Julianne's grandmother's house, someone attacked *her*," said Bethany with increasing volume. She could tell that the rum had reduced any inhibitions she had. Richard, sensing the same thing, placed his palms on Bethany's shoulders to steady his friend.

Richard tried a more reasonable approach. "Detective, what happened?"

"The accident took place roughly one mile from the house, along the Loop. You know, where the road flattens?" Bethany knew exactly where it was.

"We shouldn't have left her alone. We should've been there," she cried into Richard's lapel.

Richard put an arm around Bethany's shoulder to comfort her. "Sorry to correct you, Detective," he said, "but I doubt this was any *accident.*" He lowered his head and stared at the detective above the frame of his gold-rimmed glasses. Roberts solemnly nodded in agreement.

Bethany quickly regained her composure. "Okay, so we know where it happened. What kind of car was the person driving? Any witnesses?"

"No witnesses. Well, not yet, anyway. She was found by a group of teenagers who hadn't yet returned to their homes after the fireworks, and they claimed not to have seen anything. There is no trace of a vehicle, but we will continue looking. It's been dark," said the detective.

A deflated Bethany walked toward the window and peered into Julianne's room. Richard shook his head disappointingly and joined her. He didn't say anything—he couldn't, not yet—but he had a strong suspicion as to who was behind this. *Perhaps now is the time that I take matters into my own hands.*

Richard returned to Jade Island that afternoon. The brilliant sunshine that had recently enveloped the island was hidden behind dark, gloomy clouds. The sudden drop on the barometer was playing games with his arthritis, which made getting out of the car after a long trip on the ferry feel like hell.

His first stop was the bookshop. He grabbed a black

marker and frantically searched for something to write on. He reached into a box of brand-new paperbacks he hadn't yet shelved and pulled out the packing slip. On it he wrote in bold block letters: Closed Until Further Notice. Locals would hear the news of Julianne sooner rather than later. Knowing how fond he was of her grandmother, his close friend, they would understand.

As Richard put the sign in the window, he thought about his exchange with Julianne's doctor earlier that day.

"I'm Madaline Perry, Julianne's attending physician. Are you her family?" she asked.

Richard looked over at Julianne, who was sleeping peacefully. He simply replied, "Yes." Bethany turned her head to question him, but she stopped when she saw the look in Richard's eyes. An outsider might think that Julianne had been left with no family with Eleanor's passing. Julianne might even think that, too. But Richard was determined to make sure that wasn't the case. He would be Julianne's family from here on out.

Dr. Perry explained the tests they had run so far. The scans showed that Julianne had a severely broken leg and a set of fractured ribs. They would keep her for observation to make sure there was no internal bleeding, but they expected a full recovery with time. Dr. Perry noticed the distraught look on Richard's face.

"All things considered, this is good news. She's not out of the woods yet, but her injuries could have been much worse."

"I should have protected her," Richard said quietly to himself. He then excused himself from the room and wiped away the moisture that had accumulated on his puffy cheeks as he walked down the hallway.

His tears had dried up by the time he closed up his shop and locked the door. He was too focused to allow emotions to deter him from his mission. He was going to prove who was behind everything—the break-in, the missing documents, and now Julianne's injuries.

He used to be able to walk all over the island, but his arthritis made it difficult these days. He hopped into Eleanor's car to drive four blocks and parked in front of Tina Townsend's warm pink house. He dialed one of the most recent numbers stored in his phone. When Sam picked up, Richard simply said, "I'm here."

THE EIGHTH LETTER

January 6, 1985
Dear Mother,

We are finally settled into our new house. In fact, I am writing to you from our brand-new mahogany wooden dining room set that we just had delivered last week. We saw it in the McMahan's showroom just before the holidays and I told Clark we just had to get it—it reminded me of home, and it is like a piece of you and Daddy are both here with us.

I know that we were playing a game of phone tag over the holidays, so I'll take this opportunity to thank you for the lovely presents you mailed to us. Clark and I have been keeping busy with our work schedules and Ciarán's doctor appointments. We finally got in to see the specialist that you recommended. To our relief, he performed very well on all the cognitive tests and even scored above average on the IQ test. The doctors want to see him again before they make an official diagnosis, but they gave us some pamphlets on bipolar disorder and another condition called oppositional defiant disorder. They said that these might be the root causes of many of the behaviors that he exhibits, but we don't know anything for sure yet. I don't know what to make of these diagnoses. What does it mean for Ciarán? And what does it mean if we have more children? Will they also have these conditions? I know, I know, nothing is official yet. One step at a time.

Love,
Ophelia

CHAPTER TWENTY-SEVEN

Monday, July 6
Richard lifted a cup of room-temperature coffee to his lips with one hand as he absentmindedly twirled a ballpoint pen between his fingers of the other. He had played and replayed the upcoming moment in his mind countless times in the past twenty-four hours. There were two variations of it: one, where he steadily moves through the motions; and the other, where he uncharacteristically abandons his cool and collected nature. There was no version in between. Be stealthy, or cause a scene. He wasn't sure how this was going to play out. All he knew was that he had to face him.

He knew most locals would notice him, so he dressed as far from his usual self as possible—a baseball cap, a baggy sweatshirt he had bought on a fishing trip in Alaska decades ago, oversized gray cargo shorts, and flip-flops—and tried to blend in with the tourists at a table in the back corner of Neptune's. He placed himself at a small dinette set in the seventies-themed room, where he had a straight view of the front door and everyone who came in and out. Only a cup and a notepad sat on the table in front of him. He had been sitting there for hours, doodling or scribbling nonsense as he watched patrons sit down, enjoy their caffeinated breakfasts, and then leave. He couldn't leave, though. Not yet.

As he scribbled a fake grocery list on the last page, he heard the bells of the front door jingle. He looked at his watch: it was five minutes till noon.

J.D. had arrived for his afternoon shift right on time, just as Richard had been made aware of the day before.

Richard thought back to the conversation he had with Sam the previous afternoon.

"Your suspicions were right. It's him," Sam said to their client as they poured him a cup of hot tea.

Richard smacked his teeth in disappointment. "How certain are you?"

"Ninety-nine point nine percent," Sam replied as they sat down at the table. The tiny vintage dining table was covered with notebooks, photos, a laptop, and a box of pastries that Richard had picked up on his way over to the Flamingo House.

"So what are we dealing with here? Lay it on me, Sam."

"J.D., or Ciarán Joseph Devereaux-Harris, as it says on his birth certificate, is a forty-year-old male from Los Angeles County. He has moved around a lot since he was a teenager, though."

"Keep going," said Richard.

"He has ties to the Reaver Street gang in L.A. There are four charges of armed robbery on his record, only one of which he was convicted. That put him away for five years."

"When was that?" Richard inquired.

Sam looked at his notes. "It looks like he was released in 2004."

"About a year before Eleanor's daughter and son-in-law died." Richard contemplated the timeline. "Okay. What else?"

"Well, he's been on the island longer than you thought. From what I can tell, it seems like he arrived in March and took up residence at Neptune's when he started working there in May."

Richard stayed silent, waiting for more.

"He's been off the grid mostly since coming here. I did find that he's keenly aware of Julianne's presence on the island. I've caught him within fifty yards of her multiple times."

"Including . . . ?"

"Yes, including the other night." Sam pointed to a map of the island on their laptop screen. "The GPS tracker on his bike shows he was driving on the Loop around the same time Julianne was struck."

Richard got up from his seat. That was all he needed to know.

"Richard, before you go, I just want to be clear. J.D. could be dangerous. It is my professional opinion that you get law enforcement involved."

Richard contemplated Sam's comment for a moment. "I know you haven't been here too long, Sam, but I'm probably just as effective as Gupta and Roberts at this point. Plus, we don't have time. Julianne will be home soon. He's gotta go. Now."

From where Richard was sitting at Neptune's, he could see all of J.D.'s moves. He watched the barista as he hung a coffee-colored apron around his neck and tied it off in the back. J.D. pursed his lips to let out a singsongy whistle as he wiped down the counter with a wet rag and refilled the sugar and artificial sweetener packets. From the looks of it, J.D. appeared to be a hard worker. *Likely his only redeeming quality.* Richard couldn't help but detect a smug look on the guy's face that exuded sinister self-gratification.

J.D. swung behind the counter as new people filed in to satisfy their caffeine addictions. Each interaction with a customer made Richard's stomach churn. J.D. would always greet them the same way and flash his boyish smile for good measure. He gave out compliments to the middle-aged women like he was giving candy to children. But he always walked a fine line to make sure he didn't sound too forward or fake. Richard assumed J.D. had learned over the years how to be a fraud to get by, and it showed.

Richard waited patiently for the lunch crowd to come and go. When the cafe quieted to the point where Richard could hear the generic instrumental jazz playing in the background, he decided to make his move. He slowly rose from his wooden chair and smoothed the wrinkles in his shorts. He slid the pen into the spiral binding of the notepad and held it in one hand, while he pulled a folded-up piece of notebook paper from his pocket with the other. He walked steadily toward the counter and stood opposite J.D. as he finished putting milk into the mini-refrigerator below. Richard narrowed his eyes and waited for J.D.'s attention.

J.D. stood up and locked eyes with Richard. One look at him caused J.D.'s shoulders to drop as his eyes widened in concern. Richard's expression was one of strong resolve, but only he knew it was a veneer. He had always left "looking tough" to the pros, like Eleanor. But this occasion was different. He steadied his quivering arm with every morsel of concentration and placed the folded piece of notebook paper on the counter between them. Maintaining his gaze on J.D., he firmly patted the folded paper twice before turning around and walking out the front door. He made a point to mildly slam the door closed behind him. He had delivered his message. The next move was up to J.D.

CHAPTER TWENTY-EIGHT

Julianne was used to being in hospitals—she practically lived where she worked—but never as the patient. She empathized with her patients who found it difficult to get their prescribed rest with the uneasy fluorescent lighting and the agitating mechanical beeping that echoed from room to room. Fortunately, there was a television in her room—the room she had recently been moved into—which did a good job at distracting her from reality.

She had slept through the night and was wide awake when Detective Roberts checked in at the break of dawn. He didn't have any news to report, as usual, but wanted to see if Julianne remembered anything more about the accident. Disappointedly, she did not. He stayed for a few more minutes to not seem rude, and then conveniently slipped out when the doctors entered the room to make their morning rounds.

Fortunately, all tests and scans indicated that Julianne was doing miraculously well despite having been hit head-on. Dr. Perry told her that there were no signs of internal bleeding or traumatic brain injury. She had suffered only a few broken bones and mild pulmonary contusion (bruising of the lungs she would later clarify for Bethany). She was, or soon would be, a walking and talking miracle.

It was not lost on Julianne that she was usually the one giving these talks to patients, and now here she was, the one on the receiving end of this good news. She had seen some horrific accidents and injuries in her young career as a physician. But for someone who had never twisted an ankle or even sprained a finger before, this experience had given her a newfound appreciation for medicine and others in her line of work.

As Dr. Perry and the floor nurse walked out of her room, her breakfast was rolled in on a shaky cart by an orderly in matching scrubs. Although Julianne was very accustomed to eating hospital cafeteria food, she realized that it, too, was worse as a patient. There was something about the lack of choosing what one wants to eat that makes everything taste duller. Even her favorite breakfast item, whole grain waffles, tasted like cardboard.

Just as the orderly left Julianne to push the food around on her plate, an unexpected figure entered the doorway.

"Up for any visitors?"

Julianne slowly turned her head toward the door and saw Sam standing there with a gray stuffed teddy bear and a box of chocolates.

"I hope you don't mind me visiting. Richard informed me of what happened, so I wanted to bring you . . . something." Sam walked toward the bed, neglecting to share that they had been sitting in the waiting room down the hall for hours.

Of all the visitors Julianne had been expecting—Richard, Bethany, or Melissa—Sam was not one of them.

"That was very thoughtful of you, Sam." Julianne reached up gingerly to receive the gifts. She opened the chocolates and dove in, desperate to replenish some much-needed calories.

Sam pulled a teal blue vinyl hospital chair from the corner closer to Julianne's bedside. "May I?" they asked before sitting all the way down in the seat.

"Of course, of course," Julianne answered as she pushed the bedside tray with the barely touched waffles to the side. There was something about Sam's vibe that instantly put her at ease.

"So how ya been?" Sam said jokingly. Without thinking, Julianne smiled and let out a small laugh before grimacing in pain. Even the thought of laughter made her chest feel as if it were about to explode.

"Oh! I'm so sorry!" Sam exclaimed, immediately noticing what had happened. They usually found that jokes were often the best ice breakers, but they also rarely interacted with car accident victims.

"It's okay. It turns out that laughter *isn't* the best medicine when you are dealing with fractured ribs." Julianne sucked in some air between her teeth and held it in before slowly letting it out.

"No more jokes, I promise," they said. Julianne showed her appreciation with a faint smile. As Sam thought about what to say next, another awkward moment passed between the two of them. Sam heard familiar voices come from the television, so they looked up at the screen. An episode of the TV show *Who's the Boss?* was playing.

"I used to watch reruns of this show when I was a kid," Sam said.

"Yeah? My mom used to rock me to sleep as she watched it. She loved Tony Danza."

Another awkward pause.

"Richard kinda filled me in on all you've been going through. He told me you lost your parents several years ago. I'm sorry to hear that."

"To be honest, it often feels like it happened in another lifetime," Julianne said. That felt truer in that moment than ever before.

Sam looked down. "I think you and I have a lot in common. I lost my parents, too," they said quietly. "Not in the same way, though. My parents are still alive in the corporal sense of the word. But we haven't been in each other's lives for a long time."

Julianne's eyes got big.

"They pretty much disowned me when I came out as a teenager."

"Wow," Julianne responded. She was both taken aback by Sam's outward vulnerability and oddly consoled.

Sam grew up in a very close-knit family of four. They had great childhood memories of their twin sister, Josephine, growing up together in a tiny bedroom community in northern Illinois. Sam's parents—devout, born-again Christians—spent all their hard-earned income on Sam's and Josephine's tuition at Lake Shore Christian Preparatory, a religious school where Sam and Josephine both played soccer, acted in school plays, and sang in the school choir.

"We were the epitome of a Christian nuclear family," Sam explained.

"But . . ." Julianne said, knowing that there was more to come.

"My mom loved to play dress-up with Josie and me. Her idea of a fun family day was spent at the mall, putting us in the same dresses with matching rhinestone headbands."

"How embarrassing," Julianne interjected. Julianne had never developed a fondness for dressing up as a young girl. Much to Eleanor's chagrin, her parents never forced her to either, a fact that she didn't grow to appreciate until she was much older.

"I know, right?" Sam replied. "When Josie and I were in middle school, all of the shopping and buying new dresses started to make me feel . . . I don't know. Uncomfortable, I guess. Josie loved it, so I went along with it. But then I met some new friends at a drama camp that I attended the summer before freshman year, and I began to realize that I wasn't fitting into the same box that my mom was expecting me to fit into."

Julianne suspected where Sam's story was going. She flattened her lips and let Sam continue.

"I waited for a couple of years before I said anything to my family. But after a while, it didn't make sense to hide who I was, even if it meant being rejected. Which, honestly, I knew would happen." Sam wiped the tear that had been resting on their cheek.

Sam recalled their parents attempting to deny what their sixteen-year-old was telling them. They insisted on taking Sam to a doctor and then a psychologist who would hopefully "fix" their child. As a last-ditch effort, they took Sam to their family pastor. After that meeting, the pastor told Sam's parents that there wasn't anything wrong with Sam and that they needed to accept their child for who they were. The embarrassment and shame that Sam's parents felt created an undeniable chasm between them. Eventually, the family dynamic became so tenuous and fraught that everyone, even Josephine, thought it would be for the best if Sam moved out.

"So during my senior year of high school, I moved in with a classmate and her family until graduation. And then I left for good," Sam said.

"Do you have any contact with them now?" Julianne asked.

"No, I don't," Sam said matter of factly.

"What about your sister?"

"Josephine and I reconnected about two years later. She went to college at the University of Michigan. Ann Arbor is a much more accepting place than where we grew up. It took her a couple of years away from home to deprogram, in a sense, all we had been told about love and human relationships growing up. Now we text each other all the time, and we talk each year on our birthday," Sam said.

"I'm glad you have your sister," Julianne said.

"Me, too."

Julianne was quiet for a moment, contemplating what to say next before speaking. "You seem like a pretty special human being, Sam. It's your parents' loss, you know?"

"Oh, I know," Sam agreed cheekily.

"Sam?"

"Yes, Julianne?"

"Can I ask why you are sharing all of this with me?"

"Ever since we met, I just felt a unique connection to you. And then Richard shared more about what you've been through . . ." They trailed off for a moment. "Albeit different, we've both experienced loss of our parents during pretty formidable times in our lives. It's tough, but—"

"It makes us stronger," Julianne added.

Sam bobbed their head in agreement as they reached up and gently grasped Julianne's hand. "That, and it is always good to know when you're not alone."

That statement, as simple as it was, was that signal of solidarity, comfort, and trust that Julianne had been searching for, for a long time.

Julianne wasn't exactly sure what had brought Sam into her life at this point in her life, but whatever it was, she was grateful for it.

THE NINTH LETTER

April 8, 1988
Dear Mother,

> *Well, I wish I was writing with happier news, but Ciarán got kicked out of school once again. This time he was accused of arson when a fire popped up in the school's kitchen. Ciarán claimed it wasn't him, but he was skipping class with some new friends he'd made at that time. Without an alibi, the principal expelled him immediately. If you are counting, this makes the third time in two years that he's been accused of—although never charged with—destruction of property. Clark and I are obviously concerned for Ciarán's well-being as well as our own. We haven't told him about the baby yet, as we're afraid of what his reaction will be. I've been able to hide my morning sickness fairly well—it hasn't been near as bad as it was the first time. But it is only a matter of weeks before he'll be able to tell just by looking at me. He's such an astute kid.*

> *Clark and I have talked with Ciarán's doctors, and they don't have much advice for us at this point. Last week, one doctor said that he has run out of suggestions. Our options are to maintain the status quo and to continue to look for new schools that will take him or involve the police and allow him to end up in juvenile hall. I did some research on the detention centers around here, and they sound miserable. I don't want that for him, but we are at a loss as to what to do otherwise. I feel like our livelihood, and the livelihood of our unborn*

child, is at stake.

You and I haven't had the closest of relationships, and I know that my life's decisions are largely the reason for that. But I'm finding myself needing my mother now more than ever before. I don't know what path to choose for my family, and I need your guidance.

Love,
Ophelia

CHAPTER TWENTY-NINE

Tuesday, July 7

Julianne was relieved to be discharged from the hospital after only a few days. When Dr. Perry stated that she would need round-the-clock care for the next several days, Bethany jumped at the opportunity to volunteer her services. One week ago, Julianne would have adamantly objected to the thought, but she was beginning to let her new Jade Island family in and take that caregiver role that her parents and grandmother had fulfilled most of her life. If she didn't know better, it was almost like her family had sent her these new friends as her guardian angels.

Julianne and Bethany, each covered with a bulky cotton afghan, sat on the porch and listened to the summer rain as it lightly pattered the earth around them.

"The new windows look nice," Bethany said, turning her head toward Eleanor's house.

"Yeah, they look great. I'm so grateful Alex was able to be here the other day to assist with that. Remind me to thank him," Julianne said. She was aware that her thinking wasn't as sharp as it had been before the accident, and she had become reliant on Bethany or writing reminder notes to herself to help her working memory.

"He knows, honey. I already told him," Bethany reassured her.

Just then, the side door to the porch swung open. Melissa rushed in, covering herself and the plate she was carrying with her bright red rain jacket. Bethany popped up out of her chair to take her coat.

"Hey! I brought some freshly baked chocolate chip cookies!" Melissa exclaimed.

"Sounds great," Julianne said.

"You know what would go well with these? I'm going to go inside and make us some tea," Bethany said. She turned around and disappeared into the house.

Melissa sat down on the chair adjacent to the couch where Julianne was sitting with her leg propped up. "How are you feeling today?"

"Each day is a little easier." Julianne sounded optimistic.

"Good!" Melissa exclaimed. As she settled in, she noticed a troubled expression appear on Julianne's face. "What's going on, girl?"

"Melissa, there's something I wanted to ask you the other day at the barbecue," Julianne began.

"Shoot," Melissa said, as she snuck a bite of one of the cookies. They weren't hot, but they were still warm and gooey, which was her absolute favorite.

"Your friend who was texting you the other day? The one from Neptune's? I'm not sure . . . I mean, are you sure . . . ?" Julianne didn't know how to express her skepticism.

Before Julianne had a chance to, Melissa stepped in. "The thing with J.D.? Yeah, that's over," she said.

"Oh. It is?" Julianne asked skeptically.

"Well, I went on another date with him that night, after you all left on the Fourth of July. As we were standing there together, watching the fireworks, my mind kept drifting back to Chris. At that moment, I just knew that I wasn't ready to date yet."

"Oh, thank goodness," Julianne blurted out under her breath.

"Yeah. Wait, why did you say that?" Melissa asked.

Just then, Bethany walked onto the porch with the tea. "I hope you both like rose chamomile. I used to make this all the time for Eleanor and me," she said as she carefully poured each of them a cup and placed them on the saucers.

"Jules, what did you mean?" Melissa asked again.

Julianne looked at Bethany and then Melissa. There was a slight chance that Melissa's date wasn't the same barista that hit on Bethany the other day. But just in case her suspicions were correct, Julianne thought the truth should come out. "Bethany, you should probably tell Melissa what happened at Neptune's the other day."

Bethany began gushing over her strange encounter last Friday when she was hit on by the "new hunk that works at Neptune's." She replayed the entire scenario for Melissa.

"Wow," Melissa said in disbelief.

"I know, right?" Bethany said in utter obliviousness.

Julianne thought she should catch Bethany up to speed. "Bethany, that guy at Neptune's? J.D.? He was dating Melissa."

"I wouldn't say we were dating," Melissa said.

"What would you call it?" Julianne asked pointedly. Melissa didn't have a response. A look of confusion swept over Bethany's face.

"You two are dating?" Bethany asked exaggeratedly.

"*Were* dating," Melissa corrected her. "Not even that, really. We went on a couple of dates. Once after we got back from Port Forrester, and once to watch the fireworks." Their interactions had been brief, and they hadn't even kissed. With this final revelation hitting her, Melissa felt quite pleased with herself for resisting that kiss.

"What a sleazy, shady asshole," Bethany said, as she

took a large bite of her cookie.

"Exactly," Julianne agreed.

"I should've known better," Melissa said. "He was too charming and too good-looking. And he had a rough exterior, too, which is totally not my type. The complete opposite of my Chris. I knew he wasn't right for me when I saw him getting off his motorcycle the other night."

Crash!

The startling noise caused Bethany and Melissa to jump in their seats. They stared at Julianne, who had just dropped her teacup onto the tile floor.

"Jules, what's the matter?" Melissa urgently asked, motherly concern coming through in her voice.

"You said 'motorcycle,'" she said catatonically.

"Yes, I did," replied Melissa. She looked at Bethany with increasing concern.

Julianne looked at Melissa and said, "I remember now. It was a motorcycle. I was hit head-on by a motorcycle."

CHAPTER THIRTY

As the day progressed, the rain grew heavier and denser until it was just a thick sheet of water draped over the entire island. Richard sat on his stool in the shop, mesmerized by the loud hum of the storm. He mindlessly watched the rain slap the street in front of him, taking a break from the same intense emotions he'd felt when he finally confirmed who was behind the break-in and Julianne's hit-and-run. In his gut, he had known all along, but the additional intel he had recently received was all the proof he needed to act on his suspicions.

Like always, Eleanor was right, Richard told himself. She suspected Ciarán would show up on the island someday. *Was it only a coincidence he was in Jade Island when Eleanor passed away? Or was there something more sinister up his tight V-necked sleeves?* Richard wouldn't put anything past him.

It was the mystery surrounding the car accident that had tipped off Eleanor. The cause of the accident that claimed the life of her daughter and son-in-law, she later confided in Richard, was Ciarán's vengeful heart. She felt it deep in her bones.

"He was always a troubled boy," Eleanor explained one afternoon over a cup of Earl Grey tea. "I may not have always been on good terms with Ophelia, but I know my daughter. I know that they did everything they could to raise him right. There was just no helping him."

"You think he ran them off the road?"

"*Think* that, Richard? I *know* that!" Momentarily, Eleanor's emotions cracked through her reserved shell. "He lured them down there with the promise that he had changed. That he came out of prison a reformed man." She shook her head solemnly. "They should have never gone down there. It was a trap all along."

"Is there any evidence to prove that he did it?" Richard asked calmly. Eleanor shook her head again. Richard couldn't believe what he was hearing. "And Julianne doesn't know?"

"No. We made a pact to never tell her about her older brother. Ultimately, it was my decision. I told Ophelia that if she wanted to move back and raise her baby girl on my island, she and her husband would need to start fresh. So between us, we pretended he was dead. In many respects, he was. We didn't want Julianne's curiosity to ever cross paths with him."

At the time, Richard wondered why Eleanor had confided in him. Maybe she was fearful that Ciarán would eventually come to Jade Island to wreak havoc in his own spiteful way. Sadly, it now appeared to Richard that Eleanor had been right. Of course she was.

The last customer had left Richard's bookshop an hour earlier, before the storm blew in. Richard ushered them out and flipped the Open sign to Closed but left the front door unlocked. He sat down behind the counter, keeping both feet firmly placed on the floor to steady his shaking legs. He took deep breaths in and out and massaged his wrists— his arthritis was worse than it ever had been.

He continued to stare out at the street. But out of the corner of his eye, he caught the shiny reflection of the handgun he had taken out of his safe and placed below the counter. Next to it sat his cell phone, recording the static of the falling rain. He sighed and continued to wait patiently for his invited guest to arrive.

He didn't wait long. A few minutes after six o'clock, the front door creaked open. A drenched J.D. stood in the wooden-framed doorway, having walked half a block in the storm. His gray V-neck clung to his body like heavy cling wrap. Beads of water dripped from his hairline, all the way down to the soaked hems of his black jeans and onto his boots.

"Ciarán," Richard acknowledged him by his birth name.

"Oooh, secret's out." J.D. shook his hands mockingly. "What is it you want, old man?"

Richard stared at him. He could see Clark's jawline and Ophelia's eyes. It was hard to believe that such loving and good-hearted people could have such a hateful and twisted child.

"I'm going to say this to you just one time," Richard said. "Leave. And never, ever come back."

J.D. looked down and slowly moved forward, shortening the distance between the two of them. He stopped and looked up at Richard very methodically before answering. "Or what?" That devilish grin of his that Melissa had mistaken for flirtatious coyness grew on his lips.

"You've done your damage. You've had your fun. It's time to go," Richard said. J.D. could hear Richard's voice quiver ever so slightly. Control of this situation was up for grabs.

"Mmm, I don't think so," J.D. replied. "You see, I have unfinished business."

"What, Julianne? You failed in what you tried to do, murdering her like you murdered your parents. You have no business left here. Time to go," Richard repeated himself.

J.D. took another step closer, causing Richard to uncomfortably straighten up on his stool. He kept the glimmer of the handgun in his periphery.

"Oooh, it looks like the old lady got to you, too," J.D. said. "You think you know me? Know all I've been through?"

"I know you had a rough life. And I know your parents tried to help you." Richard almost sounded empathetic. "But ultimately, you didn't help yourself, and when given the choice—"

"My parents didn't help me with shit!" J.D. shouted. "I was a kid, all right? *They* abandoned *me* in a godforsaken rat-infested prison." Anger was starting to seethe from J.D.'s pores. Richard knew he was putting himself in a precarious position by inviting J.D. to the bookshop and bringing up his childhood. He just needed to stall a little longer and get the truth out of him.

"You aren't going to get what you want out of this," Richard said calmly.

"Who says that I haven't already gotten what I want? Well, mostly what I want, anyway." J.D. took another step, closing the safe distance between them even more.

"And what is it that you want?" Richard asked, as he got to his feet. He placed his hands on the counter, making the gun even closer and within reach if he needed it.

"What has always been rightfully mine. You know, when I was a kid, my parents would tell me stories about this beautiful island nestled in the evergreen trees that would someday be mine. They were merely fairy tales for so long until I realized that they weren't. And it was those stories that got me through juvie. Got me through my stint in lockup. All that time, I never forgot those stories of what was mine."

Richard scoffed. "You want nothing to do with this island."

"Actually, at one time I thought that was true." J.D. began to pace. "I could not have cared less. But then I got to thinking. As the heir to this place, there is a ginormous payday in my future."

Of course. J.D. was in this for the money.

"But other than a few folks who remain in my way, I rather like it here. The people are friendly. Nice flowers . . . a nice postcard home," J.D. stated sentimentally. "And as far as those who are in my way, I think my track record shows that I can take care of them." With that last phrase, J.D. stopped and stared icily into Richard's eyes. A chill ran down his spine, tempting him to grab the gun sitting just inches below his clenched fist. *If I can just keep him talking for another moment,* Richard reasoned with himself.

"Listen, J.D. I don't want any trouble."

J.D. rolled his eyes. "Of course you don't."

"But you don't belong on this island. Contrary to what you might think, it doesn't belong—" Just then, Richard was cut off by a thunderous bolt of lightning that struck outside the shop window. J.D. launched himself toward the counter and grabbed the gun that he'd suspected was there, pushing Richard backward. Richard lost his balance and fell onto the floor against the brick wall behind him. J.D. slid around the counter and stood over him with the revolver in his hand.

"Aww," J.D. said, feigning pity. "Of course you think that. But I've got the will. And now, the only thing standing in my way is you, old man. And little sis, too, but I will take care of her later."

That's it, Richard thought to himself.

As he looked down at the phone that was still recording, he heard J.D. pull the slide back on the revolver to make sure it was loaded. He steadied his finger on the trigger. "And, as you probably heard from good old Grandma, I don't play well with others when they are in my way."

Richard contemplated reaching for the gun or kicking J.D. to distract him, but he knew that any sudden movements would make him a dead man.

"So what now?" Richard asked, hoping he could keep J.D. talking for just one more moment.

"What now?" J.D. shifted his weight. Richard could sense his tone shifting from annoyance to anger. "Now you get out of my way." J.D. lifted the revolver and pointed it at Richard's chest.

BANG!

BANG!

CHAPTER THIRTY-ONE

The gunshots reverberated in Richard's ears. He opened his eyes and narrowed his focus on the gun in J.D.'s hand—*his* gun and the one that was taking his life—as it lowered to the ground. The onyx metal shined. Even in his shocked state and despite his belabored breathing, he knew his eyes were deceiving him. Something looked wrong.

Where's the gun smoke? Richard thought to himself. He'd learned in his concealed carry course that there should be some level of detectable smoke from the discharged weapon. The smoke was missing.

He peeled his gaze off the pistol and stared down at his chest to see the blood oozing out from beneath his shirt like he saw in the movies. His fingers trembled as he rolled them across his flannel shirt looking for the warm, moist bullet wounds. But he only detected buttons—dry buttons.

Realizing then that he had not, in fact, been shot, he looked up just in time to see J.D.'s eyelids get heavy as he dropped to the floor next to the counter. Behind him, standing in the entrance to the shop, was a heavily panting Sergeant Gupta and a wide-eyed Sam just behind him. Richard blinked back into focus and noticed Gupta holding a gun in one hand and his radio in the other as he called for medics.

Sam brushed past the officer and ran over to Richard. They rested their hand softly on Richard's quivering arm and said, "I had to, Richard."

"I'm glad you did, Sam," Richard said, as he patted Sam's hand. "I'm glad you did."

THE TENTH LETTER

April 12, 1988
My dearest daughter,

I know these past fourteen years have been challenging for you. You and Clark gave your son all you had, and nobody will fault you for it. You have sacrificed so much for your family, much more than I would have. But it's no longer just you who you have to worry about. Your priorities must shift to take care of yourself and your baby on the way.

Ophelia, when you made the decision to leave the island as a girl, I made a pact with myself that I would not intervene in your life no matter what. You made it very clear that you wanted independence and to start your life as an adult at a young age, so I gave you the space and freedom to do so. I don't regret my decision for one minute. You've grown up to be a strong and resilient woman. You may have gotten your determination from me and your optimistic outlook on life from your father, but your unwavering love and grace is all you. You have been the rock your family of three has leaned on all this time, through the good and the bad.

It is now time to lean on someone else. Given the details of your last letter, I have reevaluated the pact that I made with myself so many years ago. You and Clark have proven that you don't need me. What I'm proposing is not for you and your husband or your son, but for my grandchild on the way. I have made a few calls, and I am arranging for your son to be transported to the Brighton Home for Troubled Youth in Walla Walla. It is a highly secure facility that will take care of him until he's eighteen and of legal age to be on his own. You and Clark will come back home and restart your life here. I have created a new position at the foundation that is perfect for Clark—he can start as soon as you are settled. You can even work part-time until after the baby arrives.

There is a stipulation to all of this, of course. For the safety of our family, I want you to cut all ties with your son. As much as it pains me to say this, he is a danger to our family and will not be welcome on this island under any circumstances. And as soon as you recognize that his behavior is not a reflection of you or your ability to be a good parent, I think you'll be able to see that, too, and make the best decision. The right *decision.*

This may seem like a harsh proposition, but it isn't. It's a fair one considering everything you've been through. Therefore, I hope you'll give it the consideration it deserves . . . what your future deserves. Consider this a start of a new day, which will give you renewed strength. It will be a very difficult decision to make, and nobody of any consequence, especially me, will fault you for whatever you choose.

I love you, my darling daughter. I hope to see you soon.
Mother

CHAPTER THIRTY-TWO

Sunday, July 12

The morning came quickly and without a cloud in the sky. Julianne sat in the shadow cast by Eleanor's—er, *her*—house, looking out at the bay from Eleanor's—*her*—brick patio. The water waved to her as it gently approached the rocky shore below. She looked over at the trunk of the massive cedar tree where her family rested. Eleanor would join them soon, and Julianne would finally feel at peace.

"Good morning!" Bethany called out to Julianne as she crossed the small patch of manicured lawn. She carried a ceramic cake plate in one hand and a coffee carafe in the other. As she neared the patio, Julianne caught a whiff of the freshly baked cheese frittata that Bethany had made.

"Mmm. Bethany, that smells divine."

"It's a favorite in our house," Bethany said, as she set everything on the table before doing a small happy dance with her arms.

"Is Alex coming?" Julianne asked.

"No," Bethany replied, disappointment in her voice. "He has a string of client meetings this morning."

"I thought I heard a familiar voice out here," Richard said from the other side of the screen door. His arms were full of cups, plates, and cutlery. Bethany jumped up and jogged the short distance to the door to open it for him. He unloaded everything onto the table next to a platter of croissants and danishes he had picked up earlier from the Jade Island Bakery, and Bethany started arranging everything into five place settings. Richard poured coffee into one of the cups and handed it to Julianne. "Cream? Sugar?"

"Just black," she replied.

"Ah, just like your grandmother liked her coffee." Richard's comment hung in the air. Eleanor was not the warmest of grandmothers, and for that reason Julianne had always held her on a hard-to-reach pedestal. Friends at school would often gush about the warm and gooey relationships they had with their grandparents, especially their grandmas who would knit them sweaters or bake them their favorite cookies. Julianne lived in the same house as her grandmother, and yet she'd had quite a different experience. Maybe that was one of the reasons it was so easy to leave Jade Island after her parents' deaths. But now that she was back on the island, she was starting to notice more subtle similarities between her and Eleanor, how they take their coffee being the least of them. Before, she'd never given serious thought to how similar they actually were, but that was likely to change very soon, now that she had returned *home*.

Julianne's stream of consciousness was interrupted as another guest arrived from the sunny side of the house for their alfresco breakfast.

"Melissa!" Bethany gleefully called out as she greeted the petite woman with a dramatic embrace. Melissa walked over to give Julianne, propped up in her wheelchair, a big sisterly hug. While the past two weeks had been chaotic, the time they'd spent together had done one good, unexpected thing: it had bonded everyone for life.

"This breakfast looks delicious," Melissa said as she pushed her sunglasses on top of her head. Melissa, who was leaving the island after breakfast, had been spared from bringing something to share.

"I know that this vacation wasn't all sunshine and rainbows for you," Julianne said, as she gestured toward the leg propped up in front of her. "Are you sure you're ready to go back so soon?"

Melissa waved her croissant in the air dismissively at Julianne's comment. As she finished chewing, she said, "You know what? Yeah, there were some definite highs and lows. A lot of lessons learned, too. I am likely not dating anyone, like, ever again." She paused as a few awkward laughs filled the patio. "But, other than that, these past two weeks were everything that I needed them to be. I reconnected with an old friend, made new ones, and was even able to squeeze in some self-discovery along the way, which is hard to do when you have two small children always hopping around you."

"You are going to be missed around here," Richard said quietly.

Melissa reached over and squeezed his hand. "Oh, I'll be back. You all can't get rid of me that quickly!" she said, laughing.

"In fact, she has already committed herself to bringing the kids back for Labor Day weekend!" Bethany exclaimed as she scrunched her nose at Melissa. Melissa scrunched her nose and smiled at Bethany in return.

"Hello, everybody! Am I late?" Sam crept cautiously around the side of the house toward the patio. They were welcomed with cheers.

Richard stood up and pulled out the chair next to him. "Not at all, Sam! Breakfast is just getting started. Coffee?"

Sam nodded eagerly as they put down a carton of orange juice on the table. "I really appreciate the invitation. Everything looks delicious!"

"Now that everyone is here, let's dig in!" Bethany

said. They took turns loading their plates with pastries and slices of frittata. Melissa filled Julianne's plate and poured her some juice before filling her own plate. In a matter of minutes, everyone had quieted down to enjoy the spread of sweet and savory treats in front of them.

"Sam, are you leaving today, too?" Melissa asked in between bites.

Sam gave a slow methodical head nod as they finished chewing. "I am. I have another job waiting for me back in Portland."

"I still can't wrap my head around the fact that you are a private investigator," Melissa said, shaking her head. Sam gave up their fake persona as a freelance writer after the incident at the Book Cellar.

"Sorry about that," Sam said. "Benign deception is part of the job description."

"No worries, Sam. We *completely* understand," Bethany affirmed. After he gave his statement to the police, Richard revealed to the rest of the group that he'd suspected J.D. the minute he discovered the break-in at Eleanor's. After everyone left his apartment that night, he went online and hired Sam to begin their investigations immediately.

After they cleaned their plates, the five new friends sat around the table exchanging lighthearted tales, only pausing to refill their coffee cups. As they were nearing the last few drops of coffee in their mugs, two unexpected visitors arrived from the side of the house.

"Sergeant Gupta. Detective Roberts," Richard said. He stood to shake their hands. He still felt a twinge of guilt for how he'd spoken to the detective at the hospital.

The detective held a black shoebox in his hands. The lid read *Chanel*. Immediately, Julianne knew where the detective had retrieved that box. As a little girl, she would play "shoe store" in her grandmother's closet. Her mother would pretend to be a customer and would ask for a pair of shoes to try on, and then Julianne would walk out of her grandmother's closet with a brand-new shoebox and fit her with a pair of high heels that had barely been worn. For many years, this Chanel box had contained her mother's favorite pair of red suede slingbacks.

"We found this box at the temporary residence of J.D. Harris," Detective Roberts said. He walked over to Julianne and placed the box in her lap. "I believe this is yours."

Julianne looked at everyone around the table before gently lifting the lid. Instead of shoes, the box held stacks of folded papers. Some were clearly official documents, but the majority were handwritten envelopes, most of which seemed to be addressed to her grandmother. Each envelope, she could tell, was stuffed with handwritten letters.

"We didn't inspect everything closely, but we did find your grandmother's will in there." Everyone let out audible gasps and sighs of relief.

Albeit very important, the will was the least interesting thing in that box to Julianne. She opened up the envelope that was on top—this one was addressed, in her grandmother's handwriting, to her mother at an address in Los Angeles. "It is a letter from Grammy to . . . my mom." Everyone sat silently as she read the letter to herself, to the backdrop of chattering birds playing in the trees and muted waves rustling along the rocky coastline. Tears welled in her eyes as she brought a hand up to her quivering lips. Simultaneously, Melissa and Bethany rose from their chairs and flanked Julianne's wheelchair. When she was done reading, she folded the letter and placed it neatly on top of the other documents before replacing the lid. Melissa placed the box on the table, and Bethany gently stroked Julianne's hair. Nobody spoke immediately, honoring Julianne in this moment with her family memory.

Sergeant Gupta and Detective Roberts were the first

ones to break the silence by excusing themselves and retracing their steps to the front of the house. As they walked away, Sam looked at their watch. "I hate to say it, but I should probably get going, too. I have to catch an early afternoon flight."

"I should probably get going, too," Melissa said disappointingly. "I told Carson and Lily I'd be home by lunchtime. Sam, I'll drop you off at the airport on my way." Sam attempted to decline Melissa's offer, not wanting to be an imposition, but it was clear she had already made up her mind.

Melissa crouched down and cradled Julianne's cheeks in her hands. "You, little sis, just need to focus on healing right now. You are in the best of hands with these two, so let them take care of you for a minute. Got it?"

"Got it," Julianne answered, raising her hands up to squeeze Melissa's. She wanted to give Melissa a big bear hug, but it would have to wait until next time, when she was fully healed.

"It was so nice getting to know all of you," Sam said. "I don't normally become so close to those I work with, but I'm glad that I got to know you."

"We aren't just your client, Sam," said Richard.

"That's right," Bethany added. "We're friends. And I hope you'll take me up on my offer to come back and stay with us!"

"Yeah, Sam. You are part of the gang now," Julianne added. Sam blushed. It felt good to be welcomed into a new family. They would certainly return to Jade Island.

After Melissa gave a big hug to Bethany and Richard, she slid her sunglasses onto the bridge of her nose and looped her arm in Sam's. "Shall we?"

"We shall," Sam replied. Then they playfully skipped across the yard like they were two new friends traveling along the Yellow Brick Road.

Once they were out of sight, Richard turned to Bethany and Julianne. "Well, I guess that leaves just the three of us."

"Back to where it all started," Julianne replied, thinking about how her return trip to the island began only two weeks ago.

"Yeah, except I think Richard should clean up after breakfast this time," said Bethany.

"My pleasure!" Richard replied cheerfully.

CHAPTER THIRTY-THREE

Monday, August 17

Julianne pushed her backpack under the seat in front of her and leaned back. She felt torn about leaving her childhood home. Even though she had fully recovered from the accident and had been cleared by the surgeon to return to work, her heart wasn't ready to leave. Weeks ago, she'd dreaded her return to Jade Island. Now, she didn't want to leave and couldn't wait to go back.

Richard wasn't ready to part yet, either, and he'd decided to join her for the first leg of her return journey to Iran. He left a very excited Bethany in charge of the Book Cellar so he could spend the last remaining weeks of the summer attending book festivals across Europe.

"Who knows?" Richard said a few days earlier. "She might be the perfect person to take over the business for me someday."

As for Julianne, she had made the difficult decision to finish out her contract with Doctors without Borders. As soon as her contract was up, she would move back to Jade Island, which thrilled Bethany and Richard. They were encouraging her to open her own private practice on the island, but Julianne wasn't so sure . . . not yet, anyway. When she became overwhelmed with all the possibilities that lay ahead, she heard her grandmother's voice in her head: *How do we take steps? One step at a time.*

Besides, Julianne was still processing all that she was learning about her family from what she referred to as the "Chanel letters," which were banded together in one of her checked suitcases. For such a small family, they had carried a large secret for years. Those ten letters revealed the history of a family Julianne had never known—a struggling young couple, the rehabilitation of a shattered mother-daughter relationship, and the grave concerns of overwhelmed parents—one that was very different from the family she'd grown up knowing.

Julianne knew it was Eleanor's last letter to Ophelia that had changed everything. The letter that gave a pregnant Ophelia hope. The letter that drove Ophelia and Clark to make the biggest, life-altering choice of their lives. The letter that separated them from their first born, who lived the rest of his life seeking revenge. The letter that brought them back to Jade Island where they restarted their life as a family of three. The letter that led Julianne to this place at this time.

Every day Julianne thought about asking Richard to fill in the gaps left by the letters. She desperately wanted to know why her parents or her grandmother never told her about her brother. At the same time, she was fearful of what she would learn if she knew the whole story. The truth would undoubtedly shatter the perfect image of her family that was stored in her memory, and she wasn't ready for that. Maybe someday she would ask for more information. But for now, she was choosing to focus on the present and not the past.

"Ladies and gentlemen, welcome aboard Flight 1215 to London's Heathrow Airport. This is your captain speaking. Total flight time is expected to be nine hours and fifteen minutes. We are anticipating a rather smooth flight today. The weather in London is a balmy seventy-five degrees and . . . " Julianne's phone buzzed in her

pocket. It was Melissa.

Have a safe flight! Text me when you land. <3

As she typed her response to Melissa, she looked over at Richard. He was peacefully zoned in on his book. She felt a sense of comfort knowing that from this point forward, no matter where she was in the world, she would not be alone. Her Jade Island family would always be with her. She carefully replaced both earbuds and resumed her eighties music playlist before putting her phone in her sweater pocket. She leaned her head back in the vinyl seat, took a deep breath, and began to hum along quietly to herself.

DISCUSSION QUESTIONS

1. The description of Jade Island—from its natural, evergreen landscape to its small town of caring locals—evokes a sense of serenity and security. How important is the setting to the mysterious plot of the story?

2. This story is about a multi-generational group of friends coming together. In what ways can you relate to the bonds that formed between Julianne, Melissa, Bethany, Sam, and Richard?

3. Loss is a prominent theme of the book. How do each of the characters deal with loss and grief?

4. Julianne's parents are still actively present in her daily thoughts and dreams, even ten years after their untimely death. What does that say about the relationship Julianne had with her parents as a young girl?

5. Compared to today, so much had yet to be discovered regarding the mental health in children and adolescents in the 1980s and 1990s. How did you feel when reading Ophelia's letters about Ciarán's struggles with mental health as he grew up?

6. Why do you think Eleanor kept the "Chanel letters"

for all those years? How did the tenth letter end up in her possession?

7. In your opinion, did Eleanor, Clark, and Ophelia make the right decision in keeping Ciarán a secret from Julianne?

8. This story is told from multiple perspectives. Why do you think J.D.'s perspective was excluded?

9. After everything that has happened, do you think Julianne will move back to her grandmother's estate on Jade Island? If you were her, what would you do with her grandmother's estate?

ACKNOWLEDGMENTS

First and foremost, thank you, dear reader. Thank you for taking a chance on an unknown self-published author. I hope the time you spent with Julianne, Richard, Bethany, Melissa, and Sam was enjoyable and a great way to break away from your own island of reality.

I have so much appreciation for Tomi Black and Anne Ladd for reading one of the earliest iterations of this novel and for sharing their brilliant feedback without holding back. I don't know if I would have had the courage to continue the writing process if it weren't for you both.

To my sensitivity beta readers, Mar Halfwings and Sojourner Davidson, thank you for your time and energy in helping me ensure these characters, especially Sam, received the utmost care they deserve.

I owe a great deal of gratitude to my editor, Jamie Thaman. Your keen eye for detail paired with your knowledge and expertise turned my novice writing into something worth publishing.

I didn't tell many of my family or close friends that I was writing a novel during the process. Whether they knew it or not, they still supported me in all the ways that mattered, as they always do. To Poochie B., Steph H., Shannon P.,

Stacie O., Jess N., and Stephanie G.: you all inspired me to write about the power of strong, supportive, and loving friendships, especially during times of grief. Thank you from the bottom of my heart.

Finally, to my husband and better half, Brian: I won't ever be able to thank you enough for your support and enthusiasm. You are the maker of all my dreams that come true, which now even includes authoring and publishing a book.

ABOUT THE AUTHOR

Mandy Casto discovered her passion for writing stories circa 1995 when she was a student at Bentley Elementary School in Canton, Michigan. She currently teaches and writes stories in Oregon, where she lives with her husband and their dog. *Return to Jade Island* is Mandy Casto's debut novel. You can find her on Instagram and Threads: @mandy_reads_n_writes.

Made in United States
Troutdale, OR
06/25/2024